Not a Good Day for NAMASTE

A TEXAS-SIZED MURDER MYSTERY

Book Two

Keri Lynn

Scrivenings PRESS

Quench your thirst for story.

www.ScriveningsPress.com

Published by Scrivenings Press LLC
15 Lucky Lane
Morrilton, Arkansas 72110
https://ScriveningsPress.com

Printed in the United States of America

Paperback ISBN 978-1-64917-250-1

eBook ISBN 978-1-64917-251-8

Cover by Linda Fulkerson www.bookmarketinggraphics.com

All scripture quotations in this publication are from the Good News Translation in Today's English Version- Second Edition Copyright © 1992 by American Bible Society. Used by Permission.

All characters are fictional, and any resemblance to real people, either factual or historical, is purely coincidental.

For Janie.
Though heaven truly is better with you there, I'll always
miss you.

Hearing the screech of tires quickly followed by the thud of somebody being run over isn't exactly how I planned to start my day. Then again, it probably wasn't how Ryan Matthison meant to start his day either, since he was the one who'd just been run over.

In the few seconds it took me to fling open the back door, the dark blue car that had just left tread marks on my fellow store owner was gone.

By the time I'd reached Ryan, dialing 911 as I ran, the sounds of the car had faded away. Putting my cell on speaker phone, I placed it next to my knee as I dropped down by Ryan, reaching for his wrist, wincing at the sight of blood mixed with dust that covered his face.

"911, what's your emergency?" Terri Townshend's strong voice filled the air as I finally found a pulse.

"Terri, it's Misty." Heart pounding, I forced myself to take a breath. "Ryan was just hit by a car behind my studio!"

"I've got Stetson and Jeff on the way," Terri said after a

pause. "They should be there in less than a minute. Is he conscious? If not, can you find a pulse?"

"No and yes," I answered, shoving strands of blue hair away from my face as I bent over Ryan.

"It's pretty faint, but it's there. The car was dark blue and had two doors. It's one of those that looks sporty from the front but like a standard sedan from behind."

Typing in the information, Terri confirmed that Stetson and Jeff had arrived at the scene before hanging up. After seeing the condition Ryan was in, Jeff whipped out his cell phone, barking orders as he knelt next to me, opening his black leather medical bag.

"I need an ambulance in Flamingo Springs. Victim has multiple wounds—broken leg, collar bone, head injury, and possible internal bleeding."

Scooting away, I watched as the doctor secured the hit and run victim. Taking Ryan's pulse, Jeff instructed Stetson to apply pressure to the cut on Ryan's thigh that was bleeding heavily.

"Be about fifteen minutes," Jeff told Stetson. "We're in luck. They were coming back from a call out in the boondocks. If they'd already made it back to Boulder, we'd be looking at a good forty-five-minute wait."

Stetson grunted in reply, blood covering his hands as he pressed them to Ryan's leg.

"This *would* have to happen the day Blaze leaves," he muttered.

Glancing at me, his hazel eyes squinted in the early morning sunlight peeking over the roof of my studio.

"You hurt?" The words rasped from his chest, and when I shook my head, he jerked his chin toward Ryan. "Help me get this bleeding stopped. He's got another cut up by his hip I need you to put pressure on."

Moving forward, I knelt next to Ryan, my shoulder brushing Stetson's as I leaned forward and pressed my hands on the bloody spot. Muttering to himself, Stetson adjusted my hands before tending to the goose egg of a lump that was swelling over Ryan's left eye.

The residents of Flamingo Springs don't believe in early rising when the town isn't in the clutches of tourist season, and the cool morning was silent as we worked to keep Ryan's blood where it belonged—inside him. The knick-knack shop owner's face was pale and slightly sweaty, the material of his cargo shorts rough against my hands. Dust colored his dark locks a blond color, and it coated the fine hairs that covered his arms.

Even as I prayed under my breath, the wail of a siren started in the distance, and I took a deep breath, suddenly woozy. Swaying a bit, I leaned against Stetson, and he gave me a concerned look. It wasn't the sight of blood that bothered me. It was realizing I'd come upon the aftermath of an attempted murder against someone I considered a friend.

Steadying myself, I gave Stetson a nod, the siren growing louder as Jeff worked to stabilize Ryan. The ground beneath him was now a dark brown, the thirsty dust absorbing his blood, and I continued praying, pressing harder on Ryan's hip as it continued to bleed. The thick liquid welled up between my fingers. Its metallic scent filled my nose and turned my stomach.

Ryan owned Flamingo Springs' Gift Shop and had seen a steady stream of business since opening day. The store was the kind found in every tourist town, offering knick-knacks and souvenirs at crazy prices, but no one complained. Where else could you find a flamingo keychain with your name on it? Or flamingo shaped flipflops? And his T-shirts, black with the hot pink sequined birds dancing all over them, were a town favorite. Everyone had at least one in their closet, though some of us boasted quite a few more.

Ryan is the type of guy others enjoy doting on, and he loved the attention everyone showered on him. He opened his store as a means of income while he wrote a book on a new theory on quantum physics and quickly become Flamingo Springs' favorite business owner. It was a long process, he'd cheerfully told me one time as he'd wrapped a glass flamingo Christmas ornament up for me not long after he opened the store. The book would probably push a thousand pages, and he was lucky if he wrote half a page a day.

Even to me, an all-around optimist, the task seemed daunting. But Ryan was excited about it. And, as of last week when we'd talked about it over the pink mug I'd purchased to send to my pen pal in Montana, he was still just as eager. Blue eyes almost twinkling, he'd quoted formulas and theories and shown me various notes and sketches. Though I didn't understand a word he said, I'd laughed, his upbeat attitude catchy.

The entire town was rooting for him, and I didn't have to talk to him for more than a few minutes to know he wasn't an average guy. Mabel, Flamingo Spring's former favorite resident, had said she was going to paint a big sign and put it up on the Houston facing side of town so everyone who drove through would know we were home to the world's smartest guy. Everyone believed in him, but Mabel had believed in him the most.

My prayers faltered as my thoughts turned to Mabel. Prison is horrible at its best, and even though she deserved the life sentence she was currently serving, I still mourned for her and wished things had turned out differently.

The increasingly loud siren came full force at my ears as the ambulance rounded the corner of the hotel. The sound stopped as the paramedic coasted to a halt, and the sudden silence left a ringing in my ears as he and his co-worker jumped out of the van, unloading a stretcher. They ran to us, blue jumpsuits dark against the bright sky, and I was gently eased out of the way as they took over. Snapping on gloves, they ripped open packages of gauze, moving quickly as Jeff barked orders at them.

Almost as quickly as they'd arrived, they were gone, leaving dust swirling in the air and two, blood-soaked bandages on the ground that still bore the faint imprint of Ryan's body. Arms wrapped around my middle, I watched the ambulance turn the corner, lights flashing, the siren silent.

Gravel crunched as Stetson squatted down a few feet away from where Ryan had lain. With a gloved hand, he picked something up. Slipping it into a plastic baggie he'd pulled from his pocket, he stood as the first of several curious residents appeared from the alley by my studio.

Staring at the ground, I noticed that my bare feet were flecked with little dots of dried blood, my nails sporting polka-dots. Big patches of crimson stained my galaxy-colored yoga pants, and I shivered, bare arms covered in goosebumps. Turning, I went inside my studio, not wanting to deal with the dozens of residents converging on Stetson.

By the time he'd secured the crime scene and shooed away curious onlookers, I'd changed into clean clothes, my soiled ones soaking in a bowl of peroxide in my bathroom.

I heard a knock on my back door just as I finished securing the end of my French braid, and I smoothed strands of the bright blue locks away from my face before letting Stetson in. Even under the best of circumstances I got butterflies around the tall deputy, and the fact he was interviewing me as a witness to an attempted murder made no difference.

"Can I get you something to drink?" I asked as he followed

me into the bright kitchen of my yoga studio. I made a vague gesture toward the fridge. "Water, coconut milk, coffee?"

"Water sounds good," he replied after a pause, and once I'd filled two tall glasses, giving mine a squeeze of lemon juice and a sprinkle of salt, I joined him at the breakfast bar. Hopping up onto one of the stools, I made sure to keep one between us. The metal rungs were cool to the bottoms of my feet, and I took a moment to center myself, glancing around my kitchen.

The dark wooden cabinets gleamed in the bright light pouring in from the window above the sink, and I could smell the warm scent of cinnamon pushed into the air by the small diffuser on the end of the counter. Small pots of herbs lined the kitchen window, their bright green color a startling contrast against the white of the windowpane. It wasn't until Stetson cleared his throat and set his now empty water glass on the granite counter that I realized my mind had wandered. I shook myself back to reality.

"Terri says you saw the car." Placing his laptop on the counter, he tugged on his collar and opened it, while outside, new deputy Chase guarded the crime scene.

I recounted what I'd told Terri. "They were almost gone by the time I got outside and were too far away for me to get a look at the plates. Sorry I couldn't read them."

"It's fine." Stetson tapped a key on the computer, hat pushed back on his head, boot heels hooked on the stool's bottom rung. Looking up, he frowned. "Did you hear anything before that? Arguing or raised voices?"

"No." I met the deputy's eyes, suddenly finding it hard to breathe as they stared into mine. "But I was singing at the top of my lungs, so there could have been."

Against my will, my eyes dropped from his and traced his lean jaw, noting the dark stubble he'd neglected to shave. "Stetson, I know you can't tell me a lot, but I'm pretty sure whoever was driving that car meant to hit Ryan. He's way too banged up for it to be an accident, because no one in their right mind drives that fast behind the shops."

Stetson added more notes into his file before answering, throat working above the open collar of his tan shirt.

"Looks that way." Reaching into the bag he'd hung off the back of the barstool, he came up with the plastic baggie he'd used at the crime scene and handed it to me.

"Is that the color of the car?"

Carefully, I took the bag, not wanting to smudge the neat handwriting that filled the label stuck across it. A few crumbly blue flakes sat in one corner, along with what looked like some specks of rust. Handing it back, I nodded.

"It looks like it has some rust spots that got knocked loose on impact." Stetson paused, reading something on his laptop. "If you can give me the make of the car or as close as you can, I'll be able to give State Patrol a better description for the BOLO they're putting out." Placing the evidence bag back into the satchel, he closed his laptop and studied me.

"If you need to talk about what you just went through, I'm always available, and so is Terri." Arms crossed over his chest, he gave me a compassionate look, and I dropped my gaze to the floor I'd cleaned the night before.

"It's not exactly something I've witnessed or been a part of before," I admitted softly, glancing at my nails. Short as they were, they still bore faint traces of red under the edges, and I scrubbed them against my thigh, trying to erase the memory of Ryan's blood seeping into the ground.

After a long pause, I looked at Stetson to find he was still staring at me, gaze soft. Sliding off his bar stool, he reseated himself on the one next to me, and, after a moment's hesitation, rested a warm hand on my trembling knee.

"Misty," he whispered, meeting my eyes, "it's okay. You

don't have to pretend that what just happened isn't bothering you." He tightened his hand on my knee. "It's okay not to be okay right now."

Sniffing, I scrubbed at my eyes with the heels of my hands, face hot even as my stomach churned.

"It's not the blood or any of that," I said. "It was knowing that he might die and there would be nothing I could do to save him." Drawing in a long breath, I bit my lip. "I just felt so helpless, you know?"

Stetson nodded, his free hand making a rasping sound as he rubbed his unshaven chin.

"I do know, Misty. I've been there more times than I want to admit. But what you're feeling is normal." He inhaled, as if there were something else he wanted to say, then shook his head and removed his hand from my knee. Standing, he reached for his laptop, sliding it into his bag.

"Take it easy today and cancel some appointments if you can. I'll have more questions for you later, so stay around town and keep your phone on."

Following him as he walked to the backdoor, my bare feet made no sound on the hard flooring, but the noise of his boots striking wood rang out, intensifying the headache building behind my eyes.

"I'll do everything I can to remember what make the car was," I told him.

He turned, one hand resting on the doorknob, the other touching the butt of his pistol. "That's fine." His eyes crinkled at the corners as he smiled. "Just don't stress yourself out, otherwise you'll really have a problem remembering. Best thing to do is just search the description in Google. Go through the images and see if you can find a match. But again, don't go crazy on it."

As he stepped outside, his phone rang. "Blaze ain't gonna believe this," he muttered.

Lips twisting into a wry grin, I shut the door after him. Flamingo Springs had experienced little crime since the whole fandango with Mabel months earlier, so for a hit and run to happen on the very day Blaze had left town on vacation held more than a touch of irony.

My thoughts turned to the tall sheriff who was currently in San Antonio with my dearest friend, Aubrey Turner, who owns the local bakery. This was her first time to meet Blaze's parents, and she was more than a little freaked out about it. The New York native and former bull rider had grown close in the last few months, and I anticipated a proposal in the near future.

Once they were finished in San Antonio, they planned to fly to New York for Christmas and visit her family, whom she hadn't seen since she moved to Flamingo Springs almost four years ago.

It certainly seemed that love was in the air even though we were less than a week away from Thanksgiving. Usually a time for turkeys, it appeared as if victims of Cupid's bow could be found on every corner. Lacey, owner of Beauty is You Salon, was currently in the beginning of a new relationship, and from what I'd heard from Jesse, who owned the grocery store, things were getting pretty serious, not that I thought it'd last. Lacey's relationship was a rebound one, her new love interest a young businessman from Houston who thought the world of her.

If Lacey's former flame, Cody Jackson, had anything to say about Lacey moving on, he kept it to himself. Single and wild as ever, he'd recently come home with a gold belt from the latest rodeo championship he'd competed in, and I longed to have a counseling session with him. The reckless way he lived his life had the therapist in me both cringing and sobbing, and I wanted nothing more than to see him truly give his life to the Lord.

Walking into my studio's front classroom, I turned on the lights and flipped the switch for the diffuser that sat in the back corner. I heard my phone chirp in the other room while going over my lesson plan for the class. The ringtone was the one I'd assigned Brey, the twenty-year-old who worked for Aubrey, and who was currently in charge of the entire store while Aubrey was gone.

Ever since Brey had returned from her weeklong trip to Los Angeles to visit her YouTube star boyfriend Kasey, she'd been a bit quiet, and I wondered if she was considering moving to the City of Angels to be closer to him. Their relationship was what I called a puppy romance—adorable and jealousy inciting.

Kasey was a good guy, and thinking about him turned my thoughts to his business partner, Mitch. They'd helped Aubrey and me track down suspects when Mabel was running around trying to kill everyone. I'd found myself drawn to the internet star who was barely a year older than me, something Aubrey encouraged and Stetson muttered about when he'd ran into us at the Fourth of July bash. Helping me start my own channel had ignited a bit of a romantic fire between us, but he'd been distant lately, even when I'd flown out to Los Angeles to visit him in October, perhaps sensing my own hesitancy.

Spreading my yoga mat out on the floor, I turned as the front door opened and the first of my students trooped in. Pushing all thoughts of Mitch, hit and runs, and Ryan's bloodied body from my mind, I gave them a bright smile. Class was in session.

2

"Can you believe it?" Lacey asked me as she wiped down her salon's counter with a sanitizing cloth. "A diamond the size of a blueberry!"

Taking a bite of chicken salad from the paper plate on the table in front of me, I met her gray eyes. I'd taken to eating dinner with Lacey most nights, and when Aubrey wasn't with Blaze, she usually joined us. Going over the day's events, we'd clean the salon, then share supper, and since it was my turn to bring the food, I made an easy favorite—chicken salad with grapes and peanuts spread on pita crackers.

Though it was almost the end of November, the weather in south Texas was still in the low eighties, so the cold salad was a refreshing treat after a hot day of yoga.

After swallowing, I wiped my lips with a napkin, noting the way Lacey was worrying her lower lip. "Are you going to accept it?"

Platinum blond curls brushed her tanned shoulders as she scrubbed at a sticky spot on the counter. "I want to, but I don't know, Misty. I love him, I know that much. And he loves me, but I feel like if I say yes, it'll be because I don't want to hurt him."

"Kinda the old 'I love him but I'm not in love with him'?" I crossed one leg over the other. She finished the counter and moved to wash the front door. My nose wrinkled as the smell of vinegar hit me.

"That," she agreed, "and the inner voice that tells me if I don't say yes, I'll be on my own for the rest of my life. Sounds a lot like my mama. Nothing breaks her heart more than knowing her daughter is twenty-seven, unmarried, and living in what she considers to be the most backwater town in all of Texas."

Moving behind the counter, she bent down and put her cleaning supplies back on their shelf. "It still kills her that I decided to stay here instead of moving with her to Virginia after Daddy died."

She sat across from me and spooned some salad onto a plate, piling crackers next to it. "I'm not asking you what I should do. I know you can't answer the question for me, but do you have any suggestions?"

Watching her feather and rhinestone earrings sway back and forth, I took a moment to think before answering. I nudged a bottle of water toward her, noting how tired her clear eyes were. Her normally big smile drooped at the corners.

"Lacey, if you can't see yourself being happy if you're married to this guy, don't do it. And don't worry about hurting him. You'd hurt him more if you said yes and then you didn't love him with everything you are." Popping a cracker into my mouth, I shivered as the AC blew cold air across my back. "I haven't said anything, but don't you think you went into this relationship a little fast?"

Lacey sighed, scooping salad onto a cracker. "I know I did. But I'm really trying to convince myself that I'm over Cody. I thought that maybe if I started seeing Tom again the feelings would go away."

"It takes time to get over someone you really cared about." Tone matter of fact, I rubbed one hand down my thigh, the soft material of my maxi skirt catching on my callouses. "Jumping into another relationship right away only makes it worse."

Lacey nodded and took a bite of her food. "I know you're right. And I know I should be happy on my own for a while. I told Tom I needed some time." Smiling, the soft light of the evening sun shining through the windows lent a glow to her tanned face.

"You should have been there when he proposed. He took me to a fancy rooftop restaurant and had the ring brought out on a saucer of chocolate dipped strawberries. It was everything I wanted in a proposal, but I couldn't help but wonder if he was wishing I was Natalie."

At my raised eyebrow, she continued, "Natalie is a former flame. They were engaged for a while before she broke it off. From what Tom told me, she was unhappy living in Houston and said she needed to find herself, discover her purpose in life, before she committed to a lifelong relationship."

Lacey winced, as if traveling back to the night of the conversation. "That was four years ago. She never came back. She left her job, sold her condo, and joined a mission trip to Uganda. Last he heard, she was almost done with Bible school and was heading up a new mission's team for Russia."

I stared out the window, watching Jesse walk past, carrying a takeout box from Esposito's. A few other residents meandered down the street, and when I finally turned back to Lacey, she'd finished her salad and was draining her water bottle.

"What aren't you telling me?" I reached for her empty plate, stacking it on mine.

She blushed. "I reached out to Natalie today on Facebook. I

told her who I was and asked how she was doing. From there I told her that Tom proposed but that I felt like he was still in love with her." Lacey let out a soft laugh. "That's when I found out that she's still in love with him too. But she swore she'll never tell him and that I'm welcome to him."

"So, back to square one," I concluded. "You want to marry him even though he's clearly not the love of your life and you aren't his either, simply because you're both tired of being alone."

Glancing down at my hands, I studied my nails for a moment before continuing, noting I'd somehow torn a cuticle.

"Sounds to me like y'all have some things in your pasts you need to face and come to terms with. I hope I'm not overstepping the lines of friendship here, Lacey, but it seems like you've got some abandonment issues. From what I know, I'd guess they come from your dad's passing. Cody leading you on probably didn't help."

Looking up from my hands, I met Lacey's gaze, my tone gentle. "The best thing you can do is confront your past and give it to God, who holds time itself in His hands."

Lacey eyed me, tapping her bright green nails on the desktop. The rhinestones embedded at the base of each nail caught the light.

"I forgot you've got a counseling degree," she mused. Standing, she picked up our trash and carried it to the waste bin behind the counter.

"You've given me a lot to think about." Her sandals slapped the floor as she came back over. "And if you don't mind, I don't want to talk about this anymore. Why don't you tell me what happened this morning with Ryan?" Shuddering, she leaned back in her chair. "That must have been awful."

Drumming my fingers on the table, I recounted the crime I'd witnessed before sharing my suspicions with her. My stomach twisted as I remembered the scent of blood that had filled the air.

"I really don't think it was an accident, and neither does Stetson, though that's what he's telling the public. We think it was deliberate and that someone tried to murder Ryan."

"But why?" Lacey cried, hand pressing her chest in a melodramatic manner that was only hers. "He's such a nice guy!"

"Not that we know him that well," I pointed out. "He's been in Flamingo Springs for barely a year. How do we know he wasn't involved in something before he moved here? Maybe that's why he moved here. He might be running from something."

"Something tells me you're not going to let this go," Lacey chuckled.

"Well, why should I?" I argued. "A man is nearly killed less than five feet from my back door." After a pause I added, "When I called Jeff this afternoon, he told me that Ryan was still in ICU, and the doctors aren't sure he's going to make it."

"Does Stetson know you're helping out?" The direct question brought me up short, a blush creeping its tingly way up my neck.

"Not if I can help it," I muttered. "If there's one thing I know about Stetson, it's that he's just like Blaze when it comes to this stuff."

"Yeah, well, look at how that turned out for Aubrey," my friend teased.

Throwing a cracker at her, I shook my head before checking the time on my phone.

"Almost eight," I said. "I better get going. I've got a private session with a pop star tomorrow, and the lesson I've got planned is a big one."

Lacey walked me to the door and gave me a hug. "Thank

you," she whispered. "You have no idea how much these nights mean to me." As I stepped out onto the wooden boardwalk she added, "And whenever you're ready to track down who tried to kill Ryan, let me know. I missed out on all the action with Mabel."

Snickering, I turned Lacey's offer over in my mind as I headed down the sidewalk toward my studio, the back-half of which was my apartment. Aubrey was gone, so I was going to need help, and since the first place I wanted to search was Ryan's shop, I'd need a lookout.

Busy compiling a mental list of all the things to research about Ryan, I failed to notice a man waiting for me, and almost walked past Stetson as he leaned against the front of my building. Startling at his voice, one hand went to my throat, the other clutched my purse.

"I've been thinking," he said, dark eyes searching mine from beneath the brim of his cowboy hat, "that since Aubrey's out of town, I wouldn't have to worry about her sticking her nose into police business. Then I remembered that you two are thicker than the flies on a cow's hindquarters."

Moving past him, my keys jingled as I pulled them from my purse, unlocking the door to my studio.

"If you were hoping to make an impression, you missed the mark by a mile when you referred to me as a fly."

I tugged on the handle of the glass door, and my skin prickled as a cool breeze blew over my arms. The sun was a faint memory in the orange sky that was quickly changing to dark blue. The door didn't budge, and I glared at the strong hand pressed against the metal bar that went across the middle of it.

"Misty," Stetson growled, the scent of his tobacco-scented aftershave drifting past my nose as my skirt swirled around my ankles, "unlike Blaze, I have no problem in telling you to mind your business. A man was almost killed today. That's nothing for you to be mixed up in. We're short a man at the station, and I don't have time to babysit you while you run around trying to solve something that's to be left to the law."

I faced him, tilting my head back ever so slightly. The end of my flipflop touched the toe of his scuffed boot.

"Stetson," I replied, dropping my keys back into my purse, "it's a free country. I've done nothing that merits being harassed, and I have no intention of doing anything that would require your reprimand. If I choose to start my own case, I am completely within my own right to do so."

Tugging on the door again, I was painfully aware of how close we stood. Memories of what his arms felt like around me flashed through my mind as I recalled the dance that we'd shared almost a year ago at a barn bash.

"Just stay out of trouble," Stetson finally said, dropping his hand from the door and resting it on his hip.

Staring at me for a moment longer, his hazel eyes traced my face, pausing on the stubborn strand of blue hair that insisted on laying across my nose.

He cleared his throat and lifted his chin. "And see that Lacey gets the message."

Turning, he walked away, boots loud on the plank sidewalk. And for briefest of seconds while I watched him go, a smile teased my lips.

Pulling the door open, I entered my studio and headed to my personal quarters. No matter what anyone said, I had no intention of stopping.

One way or another, I was going to find out who had tried to kill Ryan.

3

"Today's Scripture focus is going to be Proverbs 15:1. 'A soft answer turns away anger, but grieving words stir it up.'"

Walking through my nine o'clock class, I adjusted poses and corrected forms, softly whispering affirming words to my students, complimenting them on their improvement.

"How many times do we answer a question or statement with words that are less than Godly? Words that could be grieving to others? Oftentimes, the person who has spoken to us has done so with good intentions. But because we allow our present circumstances to define us, we reply quickly, without taking the time to check our words. And this often leads to an argument."

Taking my place on the mat at the front of the room, I pressed my feet together in a butterfly pose. Smiling, I waited for Juniper, a seventy-year-old widow from two towns over, to stop giggling as she tried to mimic my moves. Apparently, my 'grab a cheek to settle your balance,' tip tickled her funny bone.

Clearing my throat, I called the class's attention back to myself.

"Or, someone speaks to us harshly and we respond in like, escalating the situation. I encourage you to remember that we don't know what others are going through, and grace is a gift we should extend to all, no matter the circumstances."

"Jaime, take a rest," I called, seeing the homeschooling mom struggling to hold her hip flexor stretch. Behind her, Sheryl Dowell toppled onto her back, the sixty-some-year-old having lost her balance.

"This verse is a good reflection of the Golden Rule. We should strive to always be careful of what we say, making sure we aren't being grievous, and in turn, when others speak hurtful things to us, we should use soft words in return. We don't do the whole, 'eye for an eye.' We do grace. Remember this in every setting of your life."

A loud huff filled the room as Presly, the new co-owner of Esposito's, struggled to raise her hand toward the ceiling, and the class broke into laughter.

Standing, I led my pupils in the final round of stretches.

"Being gentle with your words doesn't mean you are letting down the fences you've established in your life as boundaries, nor does it mean you're a pushover."

Slowly straightening, I released my hamstring stretch, and after a few more minutes of teaching, I dismissed my class, hands on my hips as I watched them exit. Yoga mats slung over their shoulders, their tank tops and oversized shirts stained with sweat, laughter followed them as they left.

Checking my schedule, I saw that my next class wasn't until two, giving me some time to dig into Ryan's past. Flipping the sign on the front door from Open to Closed, I headed into the studio's kitchen. Filling a bowl with homemade yogurt and topping it with berries and almonds, I carried it to the breakfast counter and climbed up onto one of the tall stools, hooking my feet on the rungs as I opened my laptop.

I opened Facebook's homepage and entered Ryan's name into the search bar and clicked on his profile. Scrolling through it, I noted that he seemed to share everything publicly. I spooned yogurt into my mouth while I studied his pictures, wondering what had led to him being involved in a hit and run. After scrolling through two years of feed, I saw a picture that had me choking on the blueberry I'd just popped into my mouth.

Two loud coughs later, the blueberry sailed across the kitchen and landed in the farm-style sink. I wiped my eyes, tears streaming down my face as I cleared my burning throat. Tapping the keypad, I clicked on the picture—one that showed Ryan standing next to a blue car that looked exactly like the one that attempted to make him roadkill. His leg blocked the license plate, and at the bottom of the picture he'd tagged someone in the photo. Before I could click the link to see who it was, the page flickered then disappeared, and I was met with a white screen that showed a gray tower that displayed the message "Sorry, nothing matches your search."

Frowning, I refreshed the page but the same message appeared. When I went back to my home feed and entered Ryan's name into the search bar again, I was met with the same list of similar names that popped up the first time, minus Ryan's.

I pushed the empty bowl away from myself and reached for my cell phone, ready to call Stetson, but stopped short of tapping his name. He'd already warned me to stay out this. If I called to tell him what happened, there'd be a hefty price to pay. I set my phone on the granite countertop and ran my hands through my hair, watching as a couple of blue strands fell to the laptop's keyboard.

Someone had just deleted Ryan's Facebook account. Going back to the search bar on Google, I typed in Ryan's name and place of residence, adding Instagram behind it. The first result that came up was the link to his page. Reading the bio that Google previewed, I confirmed that it was indeed Ryan's page, because how many other Ryan Matthison's were writing a book on quantum physics?

"I bet I know what's going to happen," I murmured to myself, readjusting my feet on the stool rungs, my left foot having developed a cramp. The annoyed grunt that left my lips was loud as I was brought to yet another gray page that said there was no account by that name, and I should check my spelling.

The same thing happened when I went to Twitter, and again and again across every social media platform I could think of. It was as if Ryan had never existed, because his profiles weren't just being privated, they were being deleted. I was certain they were being deleted by the same person who tried to kill him.

Rolling my shoulders, I looked out the kitchen window. The sun was bright and cheery as it shone on the wall of the building next to mine, but I couldn't shake the dark thought that whoever was doing this was doing it right now. Maybe Ryan knew them and had given them all his passwords should he die, something most social media sites encouraged. But I couldn't see him giving all of his passwords to someone. Unlike Facebook, Twitter and Instagram didn't need an explanation as to why you'd stopped posting.

I clicked on the red X at the corner of the browser. No, something told me that Ryan's accounts were being hacked and deleted to erase every bit of evidence. Letting out a frustrated sigh, I closed my laptop. If only I'd been faster, I could have seen who he'd tagged in that photo!

For a moment I debated contacting Facebook but immediately shook the thought away like a pesky fly. Like they would or even could do anything.

Tapping my fingers on my thigh, I wondered why someone would want to kill Ryan in the first place. I knew him enough to know he barely scraped by on his earnings from his store. Most of what he made went toward student loans, so he wouldn't exactly leave a lot behind. Possibly, it was a jealous colleague who carried out the horrific act, wanting to claim his discoveries as their own. It was something worth looking into, but I couldn't help thinking it was something much simpler than that.

Most crimes come down to money, and glancing at the clock, I knew my best plan of action would be to head to Ryan's store. I doubted it would be unlocked, but there was the off chance it was, so I pulled on a pair of green running shoes and made my way outside,

Less than three minutes later, I stared at the front of Ryan's store, surprised to see the open sign on and movement inside. Pushing the heavy door open, I was greeted with a blast of cold air that carried the slight scent of paint with it. Squinting in the dimness of the small shop, I saw a thirty-something-year-old man sitting in Ryan's chair behind the faded Formica counter.

Brows drawn together in a scowl, he painted a small flamingo figurine a brilliant shade of blue. Several more just like it were spread out in front of him, and I wondered when Ryan started selling more than just the usual pink souvenirs. A small bag of chips sat on the manual register, and dust particles danced in the air, pushed around by the AC.

The man added one more stroke to the bird before looking up at me. He set the tiny paintbrush down on a paper towel. Green eyes met mine over the tops of his wire-rimmed glasses, and a warm smile stretched across his face as he stood, still holding the figurine.

"You must be Misty," he said, extending his free hand.

Still standing by the door, I stared at him. He laughed. "Ryan told me all about his fellow townspeople, and since you're the only one he ever talked about having blue hair, that's gotta be who you are, right?"

Centering myself, I strode forward between the several wooden and glass shelves that housed a multitude of souvenirs, took the hand he offered, and gave it a firm shake. Small flecks of paint dotted it, his fingernails short and stained various colors.

"Yep, that's me."

I gave him a curious look, taking in his messy hair and trim frame. My sneakers scuffed on the old wooden flooring as I shifted my weight. His oversized tie-dye shirt said Hawaii on it, and his black jean shorts were frayed at the cuffs.

Realizing we were just staring at each other, I opened my mouth but was cut off by the stranger who bore a slight resemblance to Ryan.

"I'm Royce, his older brother. From over by Galveston." Royce paused, then added, "His only brother, actually."

I offered him a tentative smile, doing my best to look around the store without being obvious and asked, "Do you know how he's doing?"

Looking back at Royce, I saw the smile drop from his face and he sighed, glancing down at the flamingo he still clutched.

"I'm sorry," I hurried to say. "That was probably inappropriate for me to ask, but ..."

"No. No, it's totally okay to ask," he replied. "It's just ... man, I can almost convince myself that he's okay and nothing happened, and then when someone asks about him, or I see something that really reminds me of him, it hits me all over again."

Royce sank back into the creaky lawn chair that Ryan liked to call his throne. Setting the flamingo down on the counter, he sniffled. "The doctors are doubtful he'll make it. Even if he does, he'll be in a vegetative state for the rest of his life. But they told us not to lose hope, things may still turn around."

"I'm so sorry," I whispered. Gaze roaming the room, I searched for anything that might be out of place. My stomach twisted at the sad news. A stack of T-shirts yielded about as much information as the display of keychains, and the rack of flamingo ornaments next to the coffee cup stand wasn't any better.

"His right leg is broken," Royce continued, cleaning his paint brush, "and his right wrist was shattered. He also has four broken ribs, two cracked ribs, obviously some head trauma, three busted fingers, and a lot of internal bruising."

Wincing, I absentmindedly flexed my own fingers.

"Thank God Jeff was here," I murmured. "He saved Ryan's life."

Royce looked up at me, lips twisted in a sad smile. "From what I hear, it's actually you who saved his life. If you hadn't been where you were, it could have been hours before anyone found him."

"It was a crazy scene to run out to." I picked up a figurine that looked just like the one he'd been painting. "I knew these were hand painted, but Ryan never said anything about it being his brother who was behind it. Matter of fact, he never mentioned he had a sibling."

Royce laughed. "He's offered plenty of times to feature my work here, but I'm content to just send him the flamingos. I don't have a lot of time to paint much, so when I do, it's just these little guys."

Still chuckling, he looked down at the figurine in front of him, obviously proud. "I think to date, I've painted around eight or nine hundred of these things. They sell fast, and I use the cut Ryan gives me to save up for a house."

"That's a lot of talent in one family." Hesitating, I wondered how much more I could dig without being nosy.

Royce must have guessed what I was thinking. He took a sip from his coffee mug. "Yeah," he murmured. "It's just me and Ryan, so our parents really spoiled us when we were growing up." His green eyes darkened, and he shook his head, letting out another sigh.

"How are they handling this? How are *you* handling it?" I asked quietly.

"Not well," he answered. "But who does? I mean, you get a call that your kid brother is lying in a hospital bed because he got hit by a car, and the doctors don't know if he'll ever wake up."

The laugh he let out was short. "Me? I'm just doing the best I can to hold it together. I know how much this store means to him, so that's why I'm here. To keep it running." He eyed the bag of chips next to him before taking another sip from his mug. "Thank God for Cynthia."

I moved forward, fingering one of the keychains. "Cynthia? Your wife?"

Royce snorted. "As if! No, she's Ryan's girlfriend. I think they've been together for at least six years. She's been by his side since this happened. Hasn't left for more than a few hours at a time—just to get fresh clothes or food."

I pulled the keychain off the hook and stared at it as if I was double-checking the spelling. "No kidding? He never once said anything about being taken." I chuckled. "Guess it's a good thing I didn't flirt with him, right?"

Royce didn't answer, and when I looked over at him, he was

staring at me with a puzzled, almost angry expression on his face. "You know, Misty, if I didn't know better, I'd say you work with the cops, because you're asking an awful lot of questions." His tone was laidback, but the look in his eyes was anything but, and I walked toward the counter, digging in my pocket for money as I placed the keychain on the counter.

While I boast certifications in both theology and nutrition, I hold a master's degree in counseling, and one of the leading signs I was taught to study in clients was body language. Royce's arms were crossed over his chest, a defensive gesture, and his torso pushed forward a bit, which, in this situation, was an act of intimidation.

If one isn't careful, their feelings will display themselves in their body language, and I knew that if I wanted to get anywhere with Royce, I'd need to keep an eye on his, for he had trouble controlling it. Studying how he positioned himself could tell me a good deal about him, including if he mimicked me. It's another unconscious action, but when nervous, people will often mimic the pose of the person talking to them, usually someone who has authority over them or who has the stronger alpha bearing.

Even as the thought crossed through my mind, Royce dropped his hands to his sides, one pressing firmly against his thigh, just like mine.

"Ryan is my friend." Voice quiet, I stared into his eyes, and my pulse threatened to beat its way right out of my neck. "I want to know what happened to him. I'm sorry if I've offended you."

Stomach clenched with nerves, I finally found the right amount of change in my pocket and pushed it across the counter, waiting for Royce to ring the purchase up.

Royce stared at me for a long moment before punching various buttons on the register and picking up the money.

"No offense taken," he finally said. "I'm a little edgy right now, and I've already been questioned a few times by that deputy who shares his name with a hat."

Making a sympathetic noise, I reached forward and scooped up the keychain but accidentally knocked one of the freshly painted blue flamingos onto the floor. Shattering, white powder coated the wood planks around it, but before I could even open my mouth to apologize, Royce stood in front of me, sneaker clad feet covering the mess, shards of porcelain crunching beneath him.

"I am so sorry," I gasped, reaching back into my pocket. "Please, tell me what I owe you, and I'll help clean it up."

"Oh, no need," Royce told me, and though his lips were stretched into a polite smile, his eyes were hard. "Accidents happen."

Pausing, the back of my neck tingled.

"If you're sure ..."

Royce nodded. "These blue flamingos aren't for regular sale anyways. Ryan has a buyer who put in a custom order, so it's not a big deal."

"Well," I hesitated.

"Seriously, it's fine." Royce's smile tightened. "You probably should be going. I'm sure you're a busy woman."

"Oh, you know it." Voice holding a forced cheerfulness, I backed toward the entrance. "Again, I'm so sorry, and I hope you have a good day."

I reached behind me and pushed the door open, turned, and darted out to the sidewalk. As the door closed behind me with a heavy thud, I looked at the keychain in my hand. Lily, it read. I didn't even know anyone by that name.

Tucking it into my pocket, I turned toward my business and almost ran over Seth Carline, an elderly man who moved to Flamingo Springs not long after Ryan. He'd taken up residence in the empty apartment above the local attorney's office and spent his days sunning on the flat roof, learning French and managing his investments.

Voice apologetic, I steadied him. "I wasn't looking where I was going. Are you okay?"

"It's no problem, Misty," he chuckled. The light wind moved through his short, curly white hair.

"In fact, if I were a decade younger, I'd have used this to ask you out!" Throwing his head back, he laughed. The sun caught in his neatly trimmed white beard.

I giggled. "Something tells me you were quite the lady's man in your younger days," I told him, smoothing my hair away from my face.

Seth stared at me, white teeth glinting, the small gold hoop in his left ear quivering. "Were? My dear, I assure you that I still am."

Both of us laughed. We visited for a bit longer before I bid him good day, needing to prepare for my next class.

"He in there?" Seth asked, and I stared at him, confused.

Seth nodded at Ryan's store.

"Royce. He in?"

"Ryan's brother? Yes, but how do you know him?" I followed my question with a sweet smile, hoping to find something out about Ryan's mysterious sibling.

Seth scrubbed a hand down his denim shirt, patting the breast pocket before remembering he no longer smoked, something he'd told me he'd given up shortly before he moved to Flamingo Springs.

"Royce? I've known him and Ryan since they were in preschool. I used to eat dinner with their parents all the time. When I spend time in the city, I usually fill the car up with those little figurines Royce paints and bring 'em back to Ryan."

Letting out a sigh, he rubbed the back of his neck. "It's a

shame, ain't it, what happened to Ryan? This world is so dangerous anymore."

I bit my lip and nodded. "I'm keeping him in my prayers, Seth. His name is on my prayer board, right next to yours."

Seth gave me a grin. "This old rascal can use all the prayer he can get." Looking over my shoulder at the building behind me, he scuffed the toe of his squared toed boot against the boardwalk. "I hate to cut this short, but I've got an investment firm calling soon ..."

Moving back, I made room for him to step up to the door to Ryan's store. "Oh, no, not at all." I gave him a smile. "You take care, okay? And let me know when you want that pie from Aubrey's."

We exchanged a few more words, and then I hurried down the street to my business, nodding at fellow townspeople as I passed them on the way.

Once I was back in my kitchen, I opened my laptop again and went back to Facebook and searched Royce's name. When I went to his profile, I was met with a newsfeed full of new updates. Both his profile picture and cover photo had been changed less than a day ago, and as I scrolled through his albums, I saw inconsistencies that made me wonder what he was hiding.

"Ryan and me trying to impress the ladies," one caption read. "The fourteenth picture is my favorite. He's always twisting the belt as soon as he gets in."

Frowning, I scrolled through the album. There were only thirteen photos, and none of them matched the description he'd written. Album after album was like this, as if Royce had gone through every photo he'd ever uploaded and deleted the ones that alluded to the same subject, though what that subject was, I didn't know.

When I'd reached 2012, I went back to his home page and

clicked on his friends tab, wondering if I could find out who Cynthia was.

Checking the clock on the stove, I saw there was less than an hour until class. My phone vibrated, and I picked it up. It was a text from Lacey asking if I'd found anything out. I typed a response.

Meet at six?

Aubrey's?

Okay.

Going back to my laptop, I entered in the name Cynthia. Four results appeared on my screen, and I clicked on the first one, but her page was a dead end. Upon closer inspection I saw that this Cynthia was at least seventy years old and had an impressive number of grandchildren. The second one was married and lived in the Philippines where, her about section read, she and her husband worked at a clinic for the destitute.

The third profile I clicked on led me to a page where a gorgeous young woman smiled at me from the profile picture. Curly black hair pulled away from her face, her green eyes sparkled as she grinned at the camera. White teeth slightly crooked, she was biting her bottom lip as if she'd been trying not to laugh when the picture was taken.

Her status read that she worked at a zoo as a gatekeeper. Her check-in memory was Paris, and her relationship status was single, but that didn't mean anything. Few people updated their relationship status. But as I went through her feed, I found there wasn't a single mention nor photo of Ryan anywhere. And for that matter, there was no hint of Royce either, or his parents.

If she and Ryan had been together for six years then there would at least be some reference of him or his family, but there was nothing. While it was possible that she mentioned him, and it was shared only with her friends, it didn't seem likely. From the looks of it, she never shared anything privately. If her boyfriend was lying in a hospital, wouldn't she have at least posted something about that since his profile was gone? If they were an item, they would have a lot of the same friends, and it was easier to post an update on Facebook than to text everyone.

"I just feel like he was lying to me," I muttered, reaching for a small banana from the fruit bowl. "But why? What's there to hide?"

A sharp rap on my back door prevented me from trying to find an answer to my question. Sliding off the stool, I padded my way across the kitchen, peeling my banana on the way. Unlocking the door, I found myself face to face with a glowering deputy who shouldered his way past me before I could even get out a greeting.

"I thought I told you to stay out of this." Stetson's voice was low.

Closing the door, I slowly turned to face him, taking a bite of banana.

"Stetson," I said around the chunk of fruit, "before you pop a blood vessel, would you like a glass of water?" I walked past him and tossed the banana peel into the bin underneath the sink as I shoved the last bite into my mouth.

"What?" Stetson sounded thrown off by my sweet tone. Following me, his boots scraped on my floor. "No, I don't want any—wait, I guess I'll take a glass of water if you have it."

I handed him the cup I'd started filling while he'd spluttered. Hip against the counter, I studied him as he took a sip. His hazel eyes watched me over the rim of the glass. The scar on the back of his hand rippled as he lowered it. My sudden burst of confidence faded as he continued staring at me, holding the glass next to his waist. He'd forgone his hat this visit, and his black hair, mussed and bearing a hat band indent on the sides, hung over his forehead, bringing out the bronze tan of his skin.

It struck me that we must have made quite the odd-looking pair, him dressed in his uniform and looking like the poster boy for the Texas Rangers and me standing barefoot, my sneakers under the stool by the counter. Clad in loose yoga pants and a tank top that sported a cartoon cow twisted into camel pose, my blue hair had come loose of its bun and hung around my face like an alien-possessed ball of cotton candy.

"Misty," Stetson sighed, "it wouldn't matter if I cuffed you and threw you in jail, you'd still find a way to interfere."

Swirling the water in his glass, silence once again fell in the kitchen. The soft hum of the refrigerator was almost drowned out by the dull roar of Jeff's truck as he drove past on the street.

Stetson favored his Native American mother, who passed away when he was five, boasting high cheekbones and naturally bronze skin. The hazel of his eyes and the straightness of his nose and jaw came from his father, Frank, who currently resided in Louisiana, where he ran a charting boat for tourists.

Taller than me by about five and a half inches, Stetson had spent a few years in the rodeo before settling on being a police officer. Like Blaze, he'd transferred from a bigger city, though he came from Galveston and not Houston, and had bought a ranch on the outskirts of the county. His property line ran alongside Blaze's. While I'd known the handsome deputy for almost four years, there was still a lot about him I had yet to learn.

"Look." I shifted so that my forearm rested on the edge of the sink and squinted a bit in the sunlight that shone through the window. "I've done nothing wrong. And considering all the things Aubrey did when Mabel was running around whacking people upside the head with rolling pins, you should take it easy on me. I haven't done anything illegal."

"Yet," Stetson countered. "Yet. That's the thing, Misty." He set his now empty glass in the sink. "You'll keep saying that, pretending that you'll stop before you cross that line, but you won't. I know you want to find out what happened to Ryan, and trust me, I'm working as hard and as fast as I can to figure it out, but stalking his brother isn't the way to do it."

I lifted my chin. "I wasn't stalking, I was shopping."

Stetson all but rolled his eyes. "Oh really? Shopping? I didn't see you come out with anything."

Digging in my pocket, I pulled out the keychain, dangling it in his face. "I'm not lying."

"So, you're saying it took you almost twenty minutes to pick out a generic keychain?" Stetson laughed. "I saw what was on your laptop just now. Don't you think I've already gone over all this?"

Shoving the keychain back into my pocket, I resisted the urge to stamp my foot. "I don't you see getting bent out of shape over Seth going into the store. Blaze sure didn't act like this."

Stetson let out another laugh, throat working in the open collar of his tan shirt. The badge on his chest glinted in the beam of light that shone on it. Leaning so close I could smell his minty breath and spicy cologne, he lowered his voice.

"Darlin', maybe you haven't noticed, but I ain't Blaze. We're doing things my way, so keep your nose out of my business and go back to standing on your head. And as for Seth, I know he isn't sticking his nose where it doesn't belong. Unlike you, he's a law-abiding citizen."

"Oh, I've noticed you aren't Blaze," I assured him, but the words that were meant to be a retort came out with a bit of a different tone, and I realized I sounded a bit breathy. From the grin on his face, so did Stetson. The sight of it infuriated me, and this time I was the one to invade his personal space, closing the distance between us until we were almost nose to nose.

"I will do everything I can to find out who did that to Ryan," I hissed, "whether you like it or not. Do what you will. Throw me in jail. Write me a fine. I don't care." Though it'd only been hours since I'd taught on the importance of applying Proverbs 15:1 to life, I was already throwing its teachings out the door. The only soft answer I had for Stetson was going to be a slap upside the head.

"You should care," Stetson growled, breath fanning my face, eyes darkening. "Because I *will* throw you in jail. Toe the line with me, and I'll have you in cuffs."

"Is that a threat?" I asked, my voice almost a whisper, realizing that somewhere along the line the atmosphere of the room changed. When Stetson's eyes dropped from mine, tracing my lips, I found myself struggling to decide if I should stay put or step back.

Thankfully, I didn't have to choose, because a clearing of a throat from the other end of the kitchen halted our argument.

Both of us turned toward the noise to see Jeni, owner of the local jewelry store, standing in the doorway, holding a water bottle and gym bag. She often came early to read her Bible and meditate before class started, and glancing at the clock above her head, I realized there was less than twenty minutes before class began. I glared up at Stetson.

"If you don't mind, Officer, I do have a job, and you are preventing me from doing it."

"Head on in," I called to Jeni, waving at her. "I'll join you in a few minutes." Nodding, she disappeared, and it was just Stetson and me again.

"I'm warning you, Misty," he snapped. "Stay out of this. If this was truly an attempted murder, the only thing you're doing is painting a big fat target on your back." Turning, he stalked toward the back door. "You saw what Ryan looked like after someone tried to make roadkill out of him. Don't think you'd look any better."

Slamming the door harder than necessary, he left, and once I'd splashed cold water on my face to cool down my burning cheeks, I joined Jeni in the large room that would soon be filled with almost two dozen people.

She looked up from her Bible as I stomped through the door, and a smile pulled at the corners of her mouth. Sitting mermaid style, she ran a hand through her pixie-cut red hair.

"I didn't mean to interrupt anything," she apologized.

I shook my head as I checked the diffuser behind her, making sure it held enough water for the entirety of the class. "You didn't," I told her. "Stetson was just leaving."

"He likes you." Jeni's voice was soft. She closed the Bible and stretched her arms above her head. "I think that's why you two argue so much."

Snorting, I moved to sit across from her on my mat, studying the silver and gold necklace looped around her throat before dropping my gaze to the small tattoo on my wrist.

"Someone tried to kill Ryan, Jeni," I told her, rubbing the purple flower that covered the veins of my wrist. "I can't just sit around and do nothing about it. We're practically family in this town, and we've got to look out for each other."

Brown eyes met mine.

I frowned. "Am I crazy for feeling that way?"

Jeni stared past me for a moment before answering. The smell of essential oils permeated the room, and I rolled my shoulders, relaxing.

"I think that Stetson understands where you're coming from," she said slowly. "But look at it this way. He's from a big city. He's seen a lot of things that most of us can't even comprehend—and we wouldn't want to. When he took that oath to serve and protect, he meant it. And that's what he's trying to do, Misty. He's trying to protect you."

Nodding, I drew my knees up to my chest. The soft material of my pants rubbed my forearms as I wrapped them around my calves.

"I get what you're saying, but do you think I should stop trying to figure out who did this?"

"No," Jeni replied quickly. "I think you could do it a bit more quietly, though. The entire town knows you didn't go over to Ryan's store to buy something." She gave me a sudden grin. "You need another partner. I think that's the real issue here. You're trying to stretch yourself too far."

"What are you suggesting?" I asked. "Lacey is helping me as much as she can, but when you work all day ..."

"When Mabel was running around trying to kill everyone," Jeni mused, eyes bright as she leaned toward me, "before you knew it was her, you worked with her and Aubrey as a team. Three women. I think that's what we need here. A team of three. And unlike you, I don't have to be in my store the entire day now that I've hired Sandra. Ever since my uncle passed away and left me with that inheritance, I don't have to worry like I used to, so I can spend a lot of my time doing what I want. I was able to pay my way out of bankruptcy and buy my building. Now I have free time to help."

"So you could do a lot of the research, and Lacey and I could chip in whenever we can. We could compare notes every day." I ran my tongue over my teeth. The sweetness of the banana I'd consumed only minutes before lingered. "I like the idea, but if there's ever any breaking or entering, anything that could be considered even remotely dangerous, I think I should be the one to do it."

Jeni quirked an eyebrow. "Got a reason for that?"

"Well ..." I drew the word out. "As much as I hate to admit it, I do have some expertise in those fields, thanks to Aubrey. This whole investigation is my idea, and if someone gets in trouble with the law, it should be me."

Jeni clucked her tongue before pulling herself into a pigeon pose. "I think you just want to get in trouble with Stetson."

I glared at her arched form, considering giving her a push to send her sprawling, but after a moment's reflection, decided against it.

"Besides all that," I concluded, cheeks red, "I'm the one who's been trained to fight. If something does happen, I can at least protect myself."

"Are you insinuating that I'm helpless?" Jeni said, the faint outline of her ribcage jutting through her shirt.

I waited until she'd come out of the pose and faced me before answering, studying her petite features.

"A man was almost murdered. I'm all for having you and Lacey help me figure out why, but I won't put you in harm's way."

"Fair enough," Jeni finally agreed. "Have you called Aubrey and told her what's going on yet?"

Shaking my head, I got to my feet. The first few women of my two o'clock class made their way through the door.

"I'm going to tonight." Waving at my students, I chuckled. "She's going to be so mad she's missing all the fun."

4

"**I**'m so mad about this," Aubrey blared into my ear hours later. "The moment I leave town, something exciting happens!"

"Oh, wow," I replied sarcastically, placing the phone on speaker as I set it on the counter. In the middle of making pizza from scratch, I needed both hands to scatter the toppings over the garlic bread crust. "It must be so difficult, being away from work and stress and spending your days with Sheriff Dreamy in one of the hottest cities this side of L.A."

Grabbing the bowl of red peppers I'd roasted the previous week, I scattered them across the pizza. The scent of garlic and herb sauce teased my nose.

"Some bedside manner you have," Aubrey groused, but I could hear the smile in her comeback. "You're right. It's a real challenge spending my time wandering around with Blaze. He's given me three bouquets. In two days."

"What can I say?" I laughed, adding chopped chicken I'd cooked that morning to the peppers before grabbing the plate of crumbled bacon. "The man adores you. What about his parents? Do they adore you too?"

Static filled the air as Aubrey moved around. "His mom is so sweet. Welcomed me like I'm a miracle she's been praying for. And his dad? The guy is a big teddy bear!" Voice lowering, she let out a soft sigh. "They treat me like I'm the most important person they've ever met."

"You sound happy," I told her. "Can't wait to see what your life will be like this time next year!"

Aubrey yawned. "I try not to think about it too much, if I'm being honest. Makes me sick to my stomach 'cause I get too excited. Now, enough about my romantic adventures—tell me more about the case!"

"What do you mean?" Tone innocent, I slid the pizza into the oven and set the timer. "I've told you all there is to tell."

"No," Aubrey replied. "You've left things out. Like that scene with Stetson. You skimmed it, like it's too hot to repeat. And that pizza you're making. You said you've put fresh mushroom slices on it. Misty, you hate mushrooms."

"Fine." I moved to my small living room. "If you must know, I skipped over that whole thing about Stetson because it turned into a big fight, just like every time we talk."

"If you two would quit pretending there aren't lightning bolts jumping between you and just give in, you wouldn't fight like that," Aubrey said, interrupting me.

"Do you want to know about the pizza or not?" I retorted, and she uttered a sarcastic apology. "The pizza isn't for me, much as I wish it was. It smells divine. It's for Chase, the new kid on the block at the police station. Terri said his stomach is a bottomless pit, and that he's always wishing for a good pizza."

"Bribery," Aubrey said, summing up what I was doing in one word. "You're going to bribe him." She laughed. "And if Stetson asks?"

"I'll offer him a slice too. This whole thing is going to be under the guise of making sure Chase is settling in okay. After all, he's only a kid. I know I'm not the first person to take him a homecooked meal."

Plopping down on my leather loveseat, I rubbed my hand along the folded blanket where it lay across the arm.

"Vincent took him lunch last week. There's absolutely nothing wrong with what I'm doing. It won't be my fault if he starts sharing info on the case because he's hungry and lonely."

Aubrey let out a snort, and I held the phone away from my ear. "And after you've gleaned all that you can from him, you're going to meet up with Lacey at the store?" Going on without allowing me to answer, her tone was chiding. "Misty, why not just ask Terri?"

I swung my feet up on the couch and tucked them beneath myself. "Stetson has made it clear that anyone he catches helping me is going to end up in a heap of trouble. He's already threatened to arrest me."

"Blaze threatened me for the same thing," Aubrey replied.

I took in a big inhale as the smell of baking pizza wafted into the room.

"He didn't really mean it. It's just a scare tactic."

Even though she couldn't see me, I still shook my head. "You don't get it. Stetson isn't Blaze. He *will* arrest me. He let me know that today in no uncertain terms."

"He can be a bit of a hard egg," Aubrey agreed. "I guess if you think he'll follow through with that threat, you should go ahead with the pizza."

We talked a little bit longer, ending the call when the timer went off. I headed to the kitchen to pull the pizza out of the oven. According to Lacey, Stetson had left for home early, leaving Chase on his own until the office closed at five. Lacey and I weren't meeting with Jeni until six, so that would give me a little over an hour to deliver the pizza and extract some information.

Letting the pizza cool a bit before I sliced and boxed it up, I changed clothes, opting for an ankle length dress I'd purchased in Galveston three years ago. The soft pink and purple hues brought out the gold in my pale green eyes and complimented my blue hair, which I twisted back into a loose chignon. Pairing the look with sequined sandals, I spritzed on a liberal amount of a fruity perfume.

After slicing the pizza up and placing it in a reusable container, I grabbed a can of sparkling water from the fridge and placed it in a small bag next to a stack of napkins.

A gentle knock on my door interrupted the off-key song I hummed, and I crossed the room. As promised, Brey stood outside, holding a small to-go box filled with some of Aubrey's most popular cupcakes. Eyeing me, she grinned as I locked the door behind myself, my skirt fluttering around my ankles.

"Wow, Misty. You look really nice. You smell good too." Adding the cupcakes to the bag I held, she gave me a nod. "I'm making Gold Mine Loaves tonight, so I'll be at the meeting. I wouldn't miss this for anything!"

"Anything?" I teased her as I adjusted the bag, slipping my keys into my small purse. "Not even a call from Kasey?"

Brey blushed at the mention of her boyfriend but stood her ground. "Are you kidding? If he and Mitch didn't have that big YouTube event this week, they were ready to drive down here and join the party!"

Mitch and Kasey had been vacationing in Flamingo Springs when Mabel decided to try out her hand at murder. They'd helped us solve the case and made several friends during the process. I longed for their perspective.

"Probably a good thing they can't make it," I groused.

Brey fell in step with me as I walked toward the police department. "Stetson would know for sure what's going on."

Standing outside the station, I hesitated. Mere hours after Stetson told me to mind my own business, and here I was, about to bribe his deputy. I frowned at the word. Offering Chase pizza was hardly bribery.

Rolling my shoulders back, I took a deep breath as Brey muttered about the need for a breeze. When Stetson found out about this, as there was no way Chase would keep this to himself, I knew I'd be fish bait.

Brey finished her tirade about the weather and stepped forward, opening the door to the station for me.

"Have fun," she said, winking, and when I paused again, she placed a warm hand against the small of my back and pushed me over the threshold.

"Seriously," she chuckled, knowing exactly what I was thinking. "I insist."

The door swung shut behind me, and I was left standing on scuffed linoleum flooring that had seen better days. My stomach twisted, threatening to give back my lunch, and my mouth was suddenly dry.

Chase looked up from the small desk he was seated behind, and though a good five feet separated us, I could see his blue eyes turn a shade darker.

"Is that pizza?" he asked, half rising from his chair, forearms planted on his desk, holding down a stack of paperwork.

Looking down at the bag, I swung it forward a bit.

"Maybe." I gave him my best Texas smile. "Nothing breaks a woman's heart more than knowing someone might be going hungry, so I thought I'd bring you supper." Swinging the bag again, I lifted my free hand to my forehead, pretending to feel fatigued. "My, it's hot out there, though, and this bag sure is heavy!"

The words were barely out of my mouth before Chase was standing straight, almost knocking over a coffee mug full of pens as he did so. The computer monitor on his desk rocked back and forth as he scurried around the desk, one boot heel scratching loudly on the floor when he tripped and almost landed at my feet.

"I can take that for you, ma'am," he exclaimed, and after relieving me of the bag, he gestured toward the chair that sat in front of his desk. "Would you care to join me?" He gave me a slow grin. "I sure hate eatin' alone."

Biting back a chuckle, I nodded, moving past the young officer and seating myself on the hard chair that creaked beneath me.

Chase was a good-looking young man, and it was obvious he spent much of his time around Blaze and Stetson. From the way he scratched his ear like Blaze did, to the way he dipped his chin like Stetson, it was clear the two officers were making an impression on him.

Studying the deputy, I noted his short blond hair and the small scar that pulled at the corner of his upper lip. Standing few inches shorter than me, his build was strong, and his movements were quick. With a straight nose and sharp jaw, he seemed more suited to a life of modeling than enforcing the law.

Chase dug into the bag, setting the sparkling water on the desk, his movements loud in the quiet room. When he pulled out the container of pizza, he let out a happy sigh. His shoulders rolled back in an act of relaxation.

"Ma'am," he said, prying the lid off the container and bringing it to his nose, "you done made me happier than a dog that's finally figured out how to scratch its own back."

Smiling, I leaned back in my chair, the fragrant smell of spices teasing my nose. "I'm glad to hear that, Chase. And please, you can just call me Misty." Gesturing to the bag, I went on, "there are some cupcakes in there as well, from Aubrey's bakery."

Thanking me profusely, Chase set everything out on his desk and dove into the pizza.

I took the time to take in my surroundings, having been in the police station only a handful of times in the years I'd lived in Flamingo Springs. Blaze had worked hard to update it after Mason Rogers, the sheriff before him, left office, and his efforts were obvious.

The desks were new and sturdy, made of metal rather than of wood that would dry out in the hot summers. The walls boasted a fresh coat of cream-colored paint, though I could hardly see them for the posters, tack boards, and flyers that covered them.

To my right was Terri's desk, not a pen out of place, a neat and orderly corner of the office compared to the disaster that was Chase's work area. Terri was paid to clean the office every week, and it wouldn't surprise me if she took a cotton bud to the fax machine behind her desk.

If I leaned just a tad back in my chair I could see into Stetson' office. The lights were off, the room dimly lit by a blue glow that I assumed to be his monitor's power button. The faint smell of his cologne still hung in the air, and I swallowed hard, knowing this time tomorrow I could very well be sitting in one of those holding cells.

Smoothing my hands over my skirt, one leg crossed over the other, I pinned Chase with a warm look. Heart tugging a bit, I realized the deputy looked a bit homesick as he devoured a third slice of pizza, a crumpled-up napkin on his keyboard.

"Is it good?" Eyes straying to the small ink stain on the

pocket of his tan shirt, I resisted the urge to offer to do his laundry. "I tried out a new sauce recipe."

"Some of the best I've ever had," Chase assured me, pausing for a second before reaching for a fourth slice.

"I'm glad." Leaning back in my chair again, I wiggled around until I was comfortable. It was my intention to give off the vibe that I wanted to stick around and chat, but apparently, Chase took my movements a different way.

The slice paused halfway to his mouth, and he eyed me before setting it back in the container. "You know," he said, clearing his throat, "Stetson told me you might drop by sometime this week and try to pump me for info on the case. The pizza's good and all, but I can't tell you anything."

The room turned a brilliant shade of red for the briefest of moments before I busted out laughing. "Every other woman in town has been bringing you food because we've all heard about how you almost burnt your place down trying to make macaroni. But the moment I decide to give you something to eat so you don't drop dead from a heart attack from eating microwave meals, I'm looking for info?" Pressing my hand to my chest, I pretended to be offended. "Frankly Chase, I'm hurt."

I really was too. But in a Godly way. It had taken an investigation for me to do something kind for a neighbor, and once this case was over, I vowed to start being a better Christian.

Chase looked down at his desk, ears turning a dark pink. "Sorry, ma'am. His words, not mine."

Leaning forward, I tapped the container of food. "Just eat. I thought you might like someone to talk to."

Grinning from ear to ear, Chase grabbed up another slice of pizza, and I felt the breeze from his movements. "Yes, ma'am!"

We talked for a while, telling each other a bit about

ourselves. Chase, I learned, held a passion for agriculture and was taking online classes during his free time. Pursuing a career in law enforcement was tradition in his family, starting with his great grandpa back in the twenties. Two of his older brothers were in the military, one Navy, the other Air Force, and his chest swelled with pride as he spoke of them. Both his parents and grandparents, who resided up by the Oklahoma state line, ran a tractor and supply company, his dad having retired from the force about two years before Chase came to Flamingo Springs.

After a while the conversation turned to me, namely my hair, and my audience was rapt as I told the story behind why I always dyed it. Chase worked on a cupcake, having set the rest of the pizza to the side.

Biting into the cupcake he offered me, I savored the taste of smooth mint and dark chocolate. "I started dying my hair about nine years ago, and I guess it kinda grew on me. When I was a kid, my parents were all about being the perfect family. Perfect clothes, perfect grades, perfect everything. I was never allowed to express myself, and if I hadn't grown a backbone in twelfth grade, I would have ended up studying to be a pediatrician."

Staring at the half-eaten cupcake in my hand, I studied it for a moment, collecting my thoughts before answering. "I thought my mom was going to die when I announced I was going to study theology and yoga instead of going into a high-paying field."

I shook my head and looked up, watching Chase wipe his mouth with the last of the clean napkins. The smell of pizza hung in the air, swirled around by the AC, and I uncrossed my legs before continuing.

"The taste of freedom after so many years of rigid rules kinda went to my head, and I went a bit wild for a while. Oh, I got wonderful grades in college and never did anything illegal, but because I never got to experience much as a kid, I tried everything all at once. In one weekend I got a tattoo, dyed my hair bright green, and decided I wanted to live solely on what I could grow."

Propping his chin on steepled fingertips, Chase studied me as I finished my cupcake.

"I was an activist, marching for all sorts of causes, involved in every kind of movement. When I turned twenty-one, I decided it was time to settle down and get serious about life, so I gave up most of what I call my 'hippy ways.' Studying for your masters can do that to you."

Touching a hand to the brightly colored hair that made me stand out in a crowd, especially in such a conservative place such as rural Texas, my lips twisted into a smile. "But the one thing that stuck with me was my hair. I kept it pink for the longest while and switched to blue right around the time you got here. In another year or so, I think I'm going to try a soft purple."

Chase shook his head before draining the last of his soda. "And now look at you," he mused. "You run a successful business doing what you love, and you have a popular channel on YouTube, according to what Terri says. That's awesome!"

Shrugging away his praise, I glanced at the clock. There was less than half an hour left to get some info out of him. Leaning forward, I sent him a warm glance.

"I suppose. But look at you. Being a cop is equal to being a hero. It takes a tough guy to handle this job."

Chase blushed, and the sound of Jeff's old truck rumbled down the street, rattling the papers on the wall. "It's guys like Blaze and Stetson who are the real heroes," he mumbled. "But thanks."

"I bet you're already doing a great job," I assured him, scratching an itch on my ankle with the flipflop on my opposite foot. "Why, you're probably catching things they aren't, being younger and everything."

"Well, I mean," Chase bragged, and I let out an inward shout of triumph, "I *am* the one who found Ryan's blood behind the hotel and discovered he's a lot richer than he lets on. I also figured out that he hasn't been the most honest with you —" Chase stopped, his face taking on a sickly hue.

"Oh, boy," he said quietly. "Stetson is going to kill me." Looking down at the container of pizza, he pursed his lips, then looked back up at me. "Thanks for the food and all, Misty, but I think you should probably go." He stood, and I had no choice but to follow suit, noting the way his chest slouched inward, a sign of withdrawal. When he offered me the container, I shook my head.

"Keep it. I made the whole thing for you." The smile I offered him was weak. "And don't feel bad about what just happened. I'll be the one Stetson turns into garden fertilizer, not you. Just take it as a lesson on being a little bit more on your guard."

Picking my purse up, I slung it over my shoulder before pushing my chair up against the desk. "I'm glad you liked the pizza." Hurrying across the office, I was out the door before he could say anything, and as it swung shut behind me, I stared up at the sky, which wasn't even showing signs of heading for sunset.

Down the street, Seth moseyed his way toward his apartment, carrying a takeout box from Esposito's. Sending me a wave, he disappeared down the alley that would take him home, and I stared after him, an idea forming in my mind.

When Stetson found out about this ... I bit my lip. I'd deal with him when the time came. But for now, it was time to work on what Chase had let slip. If they'd found Ryan's blood behind the hotel, it meant he'd been hurt before the car hit him. Possibly a fistfight?

And what was the comment about Ryan not being what he portrayed? Was he involved in something illegal? Moving down the sidewalk, my sandals made soft scuffing noises on the worn wood. The dust swirled up from the street, tickling my nose.

Ryan told me he barely scraped by on what he made at the store, as student loans were almost crushing him. Why would he say that if it wasn't true? Standing at of the front door of Aubrey's shop, I looked down the street toward his store, and for the first time wondered if our quiet souvenir business owner wasn't the boy next door he seemed to be. Squinting, I remembered the way his brother had barely controlled his anger toward me. Whatever was going on, I was willing to bet that Royce knew.

Opening the glass door, I stepped into the bakery. An idea about how to get info from him had come to me while talking with Chase, but it was going to require a certain platinum blond and her big smile. Lacey would invite him to dinner and keep him distracted while I snooped in the store and the apartment above it.

Walking toward the kitchen, I stiffened my spine. Already in trouble with Stetson, there was no point in stopping now.

5

"If Tom gets wind of this, he'll be livid with me! Going out with another man," Lacey cried.

"Tell him it's for a case." Rolling my eyes, I didn't bother to hide my amusement. Jeni echoed me as we sat at a folding table in the bakery's kitchen. Brey moved behind us as she prepared Gold Mine Loaves.

The spicy smell of jalapeños added a panicked feel to the air, and I twisted my fingers into my skirt beneath the table. Jeni sat beside me, working on a pair of dainty silver earrings. Her tiny pliers moved at a quick speed as she wove the wire back and forth, adding crystals here and there to her one-of-a-kind creation that would sell for a pretty penny.

"I thought you wanted to be a part of this," I said. "I already blew my chance with him, and Brey's a bit too young for him."

"What about Jeni?" Lacey demanded, jerking her chin toward the jewelry maker. Her feather earrings swung back and forth as she glared at me. Blond hair loose today, it flowed down her back and over her shoulders, covering most of her glittery black tank top. "Why can't she do it?"

"Are you kidding?" Jeni mumbled around the piece of wire in her mouth, head bent over her creation. "Nobody, and I do mean nobody, can put on the charm like Lacey Baker! Send me in there, and the poor guy will be on the next train out of town!"

Taking the wire from her mouth, she gave a final twist to the earring before setting it down. "Besides," she said, looking up and gesturing toward her baggy jeans and stained shirt. "I'm not exactly bait material."

The words were followed by a smirk, and I struggled not to laugh, though Brey had no such inhibitions, letting out a loud chortle as she rummaged in the fridge.

"And what if he decides he's interested?" Lacey shot back, running a hand through her hair. She shifted in her seat, and her movements sent the amber scent of her perfume toward me. "At least you two are single—I'm not. How would that make me look?"

Glancing around the kitchen, I watched as Brey settled a moist towel over the loaves of dough after dusting the tops with spices.

"Just tell Tom to stay out of town for a while," I said as Brey sat at the table. "Let him know what's going on, though. I'm sure he'll agree."

"Besides," Brey broke in, wrapping her hands around her coffee mug, "just because you're asking a guy over for dinner doesn't mean you have designs on him. Do it under the guise that he's stressed and probably hasn't been eating good." She pulled her legs up under herself and let out a contented sigh as she sipped her drink.

"Lacey, I thought you wanted to be in on this." Jeni pushed her jewelry aside and reached for a peach from the fruit bowl.

"I do," Lacey whimpered, gray eyes wide as she looked

around the table. Her lips, stained a dark pink, trembled. "But, if you guys haven't noticed, I'm a bit of a chicken."

"Oh please, give me a break. You're telling me you rode bulls and did barrel racing for how many years, and you're scared to ask a guy over for dinner?" Clucking my tongue, I frowned at her and tugged on one sleeve of my dress. "Lacey, you're one of the bravest people I know!"

"But he might be a killer," Lacey burst out. "What if he is the one who tried to kill Ryan? What if he figures out what I'm doing and comes after me? Wrestling a bull is a world away from fighting a guy who might have a gun or a knife."

"Have dinner here," Jeni suggested, but Brey shook her head.

"He'd never open up in a public place," she said. "And besides, he's more likely to spend time at Lacey's place than he would here." She took another sip of coffee. Her blond hair hung limp around her face from a long, sweaty day of frying bacon and flipping pancakes.

"I have a better idea. Ask him over for a late dinner, like seven o'clock or so. I can hide in your bedroom while he's there. You have two bathrooms, so it's not like he'd need to come through your room to use that one. I'll be five feet away from you the whole time, and if something should happen, though I really doubt anything will, I'd be right there."

We looked at Lacey, who had finally run out of excuses. "You'd do that?" she asked Brey. "Really?"

Brey shrugged. "Sure. Why not? And that way, as soon as he heads for the door, I can text Misty and let her know he's on his way."

"All this is perfect," Jeni interjected, "but I can't help but think that Stetson is going to find out. Somehow, just like Blaze, he'll find out. Lacey and Brey will have alibis, and so will I, but what about you, Misty?"

This time I was the one with three pairs of eyes focused on me. I drummed my fingers on the tabletop. Gaze skittering from one thing to the next, I focused on the bowl of fruit, then Lacey's fancy nails as she tapped them together, before finally landing Brey's coffee cup.

"How to succeed at life," it read. "Read your Bible, pray every day, and you'll grow, grow, grow." Vines were wrapped around the words and a grin stretched my cheeks as I looked up at my friends and cohorts in solving crime.

"Give me a Bible study while I'm doing it," I told Jeni. "I'll connect my earbuds to my phone, and you can teach me while I'm going through Ryan's stuff. That way if Stetson asks, you can say you were giving me a Bible study."

Jeni gave an incredulous laugh as she stared at me. "Oh my word. Misty, that's brilliant! Aubrey would be proud."

"I'll never know how you come up with these ideas," Lacey said while Brey gave me an admiring glance, "but I'm impressed too."

"To give Stetson a bit of credit," Brey interjected, stretching her legs out beneath the table, "and I mean no offense by this, but what do you think you'll find that he didn't?" Eyes wide, she drained her coffee mug before setting it on the table with a firm thud.

I stared at my hands for a long moment before answering. Unlike Lacey's fancy nails, mine were cut short and were a bit crooked. Not a fleck of polish could be seen on them. "To be honest, it's not that I think I'll find something he missed. It's more that I think I'll catch someone in the act of hiding evidence." Eyeing the bowl of fruit, I debated on whether or not I wanted a pear. "If we can catch him doing something, it'll give us a lead."

"So, if we get a lead, what do we do with it?" Lacey asked, reaching up to twist a lock of hair.

The nonchalant shrug I gave couldn't hide the slight tremor in my voice. "If it's a dangerous lead, I'll take it to Stetson. I have to face his wrath one way or another, and it's better to tell him what we've found than to keep it from him."

Jeni nodded as she resumed working on her earrings again. Her pliers made a soft click as she picked them up from the table. "I think that's the right thing to do. You and Aubrey did that with Blaze, didn't you?"

Nodding, I watched purple clouds skitter across a darkening sky through the window. "And maybe we won't find anything that Stetson doesn't already know, but it keeps me from feeling helpless."

"Busy hands," Brey observed, scratching a swollen bug bite on her neck. Small flecks of dried butter dotted her T-shirt. Glancing around the table, she worried her lower lip. "I wasn't going to share this but y'all are in such blue moods ..." Trailing off, she waited until she had our attention before continuing.

Green eyes crinkled at the corners, she leaned forward and rested her forearms on the table. "So, I closed the store for about an hour today after lunch so I could get some errands done. Business is slow right now, so no big deal. I was walking to Jesse's to get a can of whipped cream for the bakery when I saw that someone took the For Sale sign off that empty building Mike lives above."

Leaning back in her chair, she crossed tanned arms over her chest. "I got curious and went to check it out, and sure enough, someone bought it."

Jeni set her pliers on the table. "Who? Someone suspicious?" she asked.

I was wondering the same thing.

Brey shook her head. "That's what I thought, but turns out, the woman who bought it is from Tennessee and is here to open a toy store."

Laci stared at her. "A toy store," she said, her voice dull. "How in the world does she think a toy store will survive here? In the summer, sure, but now?"

Brey nodded, lips turned down in haughty look. "Kinda my theory. I thought she must have something to do with what happened to Ryan, and apparently, I let it show because she kicked me out and told me to come back when she was open. I don't trust her, though. This is a weird time to open a store. I think she bears watching."

Slapping her hands down on the table, she stood. "Well, ladies, I think this about concludes our conversation. I don't know about you, but I didn't get any supper, so I think I'm gonna whip up some fruit salad and grab the day-old muffins. Anyone want to join in?"

We all answered with a yes, and when I headed home an hour later, I was stuffed to the brim with watermelon, strawberries, and two banana oatmeal muffins. Bidding my friends goodnight, I watched Lacey cross the street to her salon and Jeni turn toward her store. Brey lived on the opposite side of town and her phone screen lit up her face as she texted someone.

Thoughts turning to Lacey, I replayed the conversation we'd had before parting ways. Though she claimed she loved Tom and was going to accept his proposal despite his ex-fiancée still being in love with him, I knew she was faltering in that decision now that Cody was back in town, and I'd said as much to her. The blush that colored her cheeks had been answer enough, and I clucked my tongue when she started to protest.

"My door's always open when you want to talk about the whole thing, from start to finish," I told her. "But unless you're willing to be completely honest with me, and, more importantly, yourself, don't come." I hugged her to take away the sting my words had carried. I left, hoping she'd take my words to heart.

As I ambled to my shop, I stared up at the night sky. A cool breeze made its way down the road from the desert, sending a piece of paper past me. Skittering down the street, it came to a stop in front of Ryan's store. I stared at the building's dark windows for a moment before lifting my gaze to the second floor. A lone lamp lit one of the small windows. Royce looked out at me. Our eyes met and held for a long moment before he lifted his hand in a short wave and disappeared. The light went out shortly after.

I'd never felt anything but safe in Flamingo Springs, except for when Mabel had been on her rampage, but now, a shiver went down my spine, and I hotfooted it to my store, almost dropping my keys as I struggled to unlock the door. Royce's actions seemed harmless, almost friendly, but for some reason they bothered me. It was like he was watching me, and I hated the icky feeling it gave me.

That night, after double checking to make sure both doors to my building were locked, I placed a chair under the handle of the door that led to my personal quarters and made sure all my windows were tightly shut and secured. As much fun as a case could be, I reminded myself that a would-be-killer was still on loose, and, just like with Mabel, they were most likely unstable and could strike again.

PLACING the mop back in the bucket, I swished it around in the sudsy water. The smell of the lime and tea tree essential oil I'd added to it gave the room a clean smell. Lacey had just called to let me know Royce accepted her offer of dinner for that night, and Brey confirmed that she would indeed hide in Lacey's bedroom.

Since I had the day off—my only appointment canceling due to the fact she was giving birth at the moment—I pulled out my cleaning supplies and gave my studio one of its thrice weekly cleanings. The windows sparkled in the mid-morning sun that sent heat waves dancing along the tops of the metal canopy over the upper windows of Ryan's store. All I had left to do was finish mopping, and the studio would be clean, including the oil diffuser, which was currently draining on a pile of towels in the kitchen.

Personal quarters already tidied, I had little to do until evening came. My only other task was grocery shopping. When I'd washed the fridge, I found I was out of pretty much all produce, and since today was Saturday, I knew Jesse would be stocking all of my favorites.

Humming as I mopped, I swung my hips and threw my arms in the air to a beat that only I could hear, the smooth flooring cool to my bare feet. When a sharp rap came to the front door, I was midway through swinging the mop around in a do-si-do, and I fell off balance, almost stepping in my bucket of mop water.

I glared at the door, already knowing who it was. Terri had sent me a text earlier to warn me that Stetson was in a mood.

He didn't say a word.

She'd added a confused emoji.

Just grinned. That's all he did. Grinned. Then he told Chase to step up his game or he'd send him back to where he came from.

Though I'd told my friend I was sure everything was fine,

the bravado I'd felt while texting her was suddenly gone. Movements measured, I placed the mop back in the bucket and wiped my slightly sweaty palms on my thighs. The orange bohemian pants and bright purple tank top I wore were a cheery contrast to the storm that was waiting outside the door.

Padding across the squeaky-clean floor, I avoided a few wet streaks and unlocked the door. Jeff waved at me as he drove past with a hound dog sitting next to him in the cab of his old truck. Seth crossed the street after he passed.

Opening the door, I stepped back and allowed Stetson to enter, watching him take his hat off as he did so. I stood before him, working to keep my hands loose at my side even though I wanted to clasp them in front of me, feeling much like a child who is about to receive a scolding—and a well-deserved one at that.

Stetson nodded at me, hazel eyes narrow, pupils enlarging as they adjusted to the change in light.

"You know why I'm here," he said quietly.

I dropped my gaze to his dusty boots. A faint outline of dirt sat on the floor around them and I gritted my teeth. "I do, and I'm sorry, but I've been too busy today. I can make you one, too, this afternoon if you want."

Stetson blinked, holding his hat by his side. "What?"

"The pizza," I explained. "That's what this is about, isn't it? You want me to make you a pizza. I have to admit, I'm thinking about entering it into a contest."

Stetson looked bemused. "No, I don't want you to make me a pizza—" Biting off the last word, he tapped his right foot on the floor. "And you know that's not why I'm here. Misty, you bribed an officer of the law. Do you have any idea how serious of a charge that is?"

Turning away from him, I moved back to my mop.

"I didn't bribe him," I said over my shoulder. "I took Chase supper because I heard how hungry he's been. Every woman in town has been doing it, Aubrey included, and I don't see you harassing her about it."

Stetson followed me, and I resisted the urge to hit him over the head with the wet end of the mop. "Chase confessed to telling you about the case. How you got him all comfortable and relaxed."

I made my way back to the door and mopped up the dusty boot prints he left, letting out a huff as I slapped the wet strands of cloth against his heels. He turned and stared at me like I'd lost my mind.

"I took him supper, Stetson, and we talked about our families. There was no bribing. If he starts spilling confidential info because he got comfortable, you better never let that boy around alcohol."

Stetson blew out a loud breath and ran a hand through his dark hair. "Woman," he ground out through gritted teeth and slapped his hat against his blue-jeaned thigh, "I know what you're up to. Sooner or later, you're going to make a mistake, and I'm going to slam you with everything I can. Don't think I haven't been building a case against you."

Pushing the mop forward, I rested it on his right boot, dampening the cuff of his pants.

"Deputy," I said, swishing the mop back and forth, determined to stop the dirt from getting on my clean floors since he kept walking all over them, "don't you have bigger things to worry about, like solving this case or training your employee?"

I moved the mop to the other boot, and before I could blink, my hands were trapped under Stetson's, freezing the mop where it was. Hat now on the floor, Stetson leaned forward, lips parting in a grin that sent a shiver right down to my toes.

"Misty, I saw your face when you came to the door. You're

scared spitless right now. You don't fool me. You toed the line last night, but sooner or later, you'll cross it. In some ways, you already have."

Giving the mop a sudden tug, he stepped forward and I stumbled, catching myself right before my nose planted in his chest. I struggled to get my hands out from under his, but he tightened his grip, and I glared up at him.

"Well it's not like Royce is going to talk to you," I snarled. "You already gave him a bad impression."

"So, you figured you'd just deputize yourself and accomplish what I apparently cannot?" Stetson asked. A twinkle came to his eyes, and I swallowed hard, feeling like I'd fallen into a trap. "What else have you got going, Misty? What else do you have planned?" The laugh he uttered was low, and this close to him I could see flecks of green in his eyes. "Why don't we just join forces? That's what you want, isn't it?"

Giving another tug on the mop handle, he dragged me closer, and I could smell gun oil on him. Tilting his head down to look me in the eye, I noticed the small scar that ran through his right eyebrow. Something in my stomach tightened.

"Why do you insist on doing this?" His tone now lacked any hint of anger. "Why do you insist on putting a target on your back?" Lips thinning, he cut me off when I started to speak. "This isn't like it was with Aubrey, Misty. This is different. And every time you do something else, you put yourself in more danger. People like the ones who tried to kill Ryan don't play around. If they'd attack him, what makes you think they won't do the same to you. Why can't you understand that?"

I stared at his chin as he spoke, finally meeting his eyes when he asked the last question. "I do get that, Stetson, but I can't just sit by. I can't. I care too much about people to wait.

I'm not doing anything wrong, nor am I not doing anything illegal."

"*Yet,*" I silently told myself, but that was neither here nor there.

"Nothing I say will convince you, will it?" Stetson asked. "No matter how much I shout, no matter how much I threaten, you aren't going to give this up, even if I fine you. I get now what Blaze had to deal with when it was Aubrey in your place." Voice lowering, his eyes darkened. "Why do you insist on driving me crazy, Misty?"

This time I was the one to pull on the mop handle, and Stetson leaned down so that our faces were inches apart. "Driving you crazy isn't my intention," I whispered apologetically. "But Stetson, you have to give me a little more credit. I'm not stupid. I'm not about to throw myself in harm's way. If I find anything, just like Aubrey did, I'll come straight to the people who need to know."

Stetson leaned even closer, and after a moment's consideration, I did the same, closing the space between us. Eyes fluttering closed, our lips brushed, Stetson's sudden inhale mirroring mine as the sparks of two years of attraction began to ignite.

The sound of his phone ringing jarred us, and we both jerked back. Disappointment filled me. Stetson met my eyes and held them for the duration of three rings before releasing his hold on my hands. Grabbing his phone from its case, he answered it, voice curt, authority evident even in just a few words.

"This is Stetson."

Listening intently, he looked past me, drawing his mouth to one side, eyes squinting a bit as he gazed out at the street. "Thanks. I'll have an officer there by supper."

Tapping the phone's screen, he slid it back onto its clip. "That was the hospital in Houston. Ryan's awake."

"Praise God," I breathed, reaching a hand up to push my hair out of my face. Strands stuck to my sweaty forehead. "Is he lucid? Royce said they weren't sure he'd make it."

Stetson nodded, resting one hand on his gun belt even as he leaned down to grab his hat. Placing it on his head, he said, "They've got an officer stationed outside his room since this is consider an attempted murder. He's not out of the woods yet, though. Relapses are common, so hopefully he's still hanging on when Terri gets there, and we'll find out who did it, or at least get some pointers toward the person."

He moved toward the doors, and I followed him, mop trailing behind me. I completely forgot to be mad about the dirt he was leaving behind. "Terri? Why aren't you going?"

Stetson turned and faced me, one hand on the door handle. "We're already short Blaze. If I leave and something happens, you'd have to rely on Chase." He winced even as the words left his mouth as if he knew how much of a disaster that would be. "No, I'll stay here and take over Terri's duties."

"It probably is better to send her," I agreed, stopping several safe feet away from him. "Ryan let me know how much he likes her, so he'll be more likely to open up to her than to you, especially since she's just like having your grandma around." It was in me to ask if I could go with her, but decided at the last moment it would probably be an unwise move.

Stetson pushed the door open. "Well, either way, I think we're about to get a break in the case." Looking over his shoulder, he frowned. "Just be careful, okay?"

Before I could reply he was gone, but I still whispered the words in the empty room. "I will."

Though I was unsure about what had just happened, I wasn't

going to waste time trying to figure it out. Stetson came to my studio with the intent to cower me but ended up giving in, at least to my snooping. Just like Blaze warned Aubrey, though, I knew if I stepped over the line, he would arrest me—and rightfully so.

The thought did give me a definite pause, and I almost reconsidered breaking into Ryan's shop and apartment. I set my jaw and quickly re-mopped the room. A slight flush rose to my cheeks as I remembered how Stetson grabbed the mop, trapping me. With this new turn of events, he'd be so busy covering for Terri that he wouldn't have time to monitor me, and I wondered if I wasn't receiving a bit of help from above.

The thought seemed almost blasphemous, but I sent up a prayer of thanks anyway.

I SPENT the remainder of the day buying groceries and filming a new video for my channel, an hour-long session that left me sweaty and worn out. As I set to work editing it, a task that would take more than four hours to complete, my thoughts wandered to Royce and the secrets I knew he was holding. Though he seemed to be just as nice and talented as his brother, there was a worldliness about him that bothered me— an air that suggested he knew something I didn't, and it amused him.

That thought stayed in the back of my mind for the duration of the day, and once I'd clicked the button to start the process of uploading my video to YouTube, I sent a quick text to Mitch. It'd been almost a day since we'd last had contact with each other, and I asked how the event had gone so far.

Things were cooling off between us. I smiled when he immediately texted me back. After filling him in on what was going on, he asked a few questions before sharing his thoughts with me.

Let's just presume the person who ran him over knew him.

He followed that text with another.

It's extensive, but it sure would be nice to get a listing of everyone he knew and what cars are licensed to them.

We'd determined the day before what kind of car I'd seen— a Dodge Avenger, probably eight or nine years old, with an extended spoiler on the back. While there were plenty of them in the world, only one would match the rust sample Stetson collected. A cast had also been made of the tire prints and would match the tread to the tires on the car.

Mitch stopped texting after that suggestion, his class moving to a no-phones-allowed session, but he'd given me a lot to chew on. After almost an hour of debating it, I forwarded his text to Stetson. He replied via text.

Had the same thought this morning.

Looking into it right now. If you can think of any names, let me know ASAP.

Frowning at my phone, I sat at the counter in my kitchen. My laptop whirred softly in front of me as it updated. A bit disappointed that he'd already thought of that, my scowl quickly turned into a smile when minutes later, he texted me a cowboy emoji.

Not sure how to respond to it, I opted to not reply. After eating a light supper, I donned jeans and a dark T-shirt. I made my way across the street and down the alley by Aubrey's bakery. Brey let me in the back door and showed me the pepper spray hidden in one of her pockets. After helping her close the store up and getting everything clean, we waited in grim silence.

When Jeni called to start my Bible study, twenty minutes before Royce was to be at Lacey's, I gave Brey a tight smile. It was showtime.

6

I stood on the landing outside Ryan's apartment, pulling a crowbar from my backpack.

"And so," Jeni droned in my ear, "while we will probably never know what the thorn in the Apostle Paul's side was, we can grasp onto the wonderful reassurance that God's grace is truly sufficient for all our trials."

The door in front of me finally gave way as its jam splintered with an alarmingly loud crack. Letting out a quiet hiss, I was certain someone heard, but after waiting a moment, it was clear no one had. It was pushing seven thirty, so the town was closed down, and the store owners were tucked safely away in their homes.

Since Flamingo Springs boasted no bars or breweries, and the nearest theater was an hour away, we didn't have much going for night life. While that could sometimes be a bother, tonight I was thankful for it.

Stetson was down at the office along with Chase, but I knew they wouldn't pose a problem. A brush fire had been reported earlier that day out at Jamie's ranch, and Stetson had just returned from helping put it out. It had spread to a barn and done quite a bit of damage, leaving him with a stack of paperwork to fill out.

Jamie called me to let me know she wouldn't be in for her Monday appointment as that was when the insurance agent would be out to assess the damage, and she spent a good half hour talking my ear off. While I was saddened for the stress the fire caused her and her family, I was also glad, as it made my job of breaking and entering a lot easier.

"Are you listening?" Jeni demanded. When I answered with an affirmative, she cleared her throat and moved on to discuss the attributes of God's never-ending grace and love. As she quoted Scripture and broke down the meanings of Greek words, I eased the back door to Ryan's apartment the rest of the way open. The smell of paint mixed with stale coffee filled the air, and I wrinkled my nose as I peered in.

Jeni and I had agreed earlier that it probably made more sense to start with Ryan's personal quarters rather than his professional, and I took a deep breath as I stepped over the threshold. The black beanie I wore irritated my forehead, but I didn't dare scratch it. If I lost a strand of hair while snooping around it would be pretty easy to match to me, as I was the only person in town with blue hair. I'd been sure to thoroughly lint roller my clothes before I left my apartment.

Jeni chattered away in my ear through the ear bud tucked into it. My mind grabbed onto bits and pieces of the main points while I crept into Ryan's living room. The latex gloves I wore made no sound as I pressed the power button on his computer that sat on a small wooden desk held together with duct tape. The screen flickered before turning a soft green that quickly changed to a picture of a waterfall. A small line of words appeared across the middle of the screen. I was thankful it was still light enough out that Ryan's apartment was illuminated by sunlight so no one outside could see the computer's glow.

Whether it was numerical or alphabetical, I had no clue what Ryan's password might be, but when I looked down at the floor, forehead wrinkled in concentration, my attention was caught by the overflowing wastebasket beneath the desk. The pieces of paper on the top layer of trash and those on the floor were covered in numbers. I scooped them up, laying them out on the desk.

The first one I looked at had the words "Phone PW" scrawled across the top in dark blue ink. Looking at the sloppy columns that covered the front and back of the page, I realized someone was desperate to unlock a phone. Only three of the multiple rows of numbers had little *X's* next to them. It was my guess that whoever was trying to unlock the phone had given up, as they'd either received a warning that a fourth attempt would reset the phone, or they realized how long it might take them to figure out the code.

Glancing back at the computer screen, Jeni still yakking away, pausing now and then to take a sip of coffee, I tapped the space bar. A white text box appeared, requesting a pin number, and I checked the papers again. It would be just like Ryan to use numerical codes for everything. Sifting through the stack, I stopped when I found one titled "Email PW." It was another sloppily filled page, the ink so dark and jagged about halfway through I knew whoever was trying to get into the account had gotten irritated.

It was clear from how many of the codes had been checked off that they wanted to hack the email first. Emails are often linked to cell phones, and, depending on the setup, one could change the pin of a phone through email, after a lengthy series of questions.

"This is crazy," I muttered, and Jeni paused in stating the

importance of trusting only in God.

"Need help?" she asked.

"No." I hesitated. "It looks like someone has spent a lot of time trying to get into Ryan's email account. From there, they could reset the password on his phone, and after that, getting into the computer would be easy. Just enter the wrong password three times, and you'll get a text from the computer asking if you want to reset your password."

"Does it look like they succeeded?" Jeni asked quietly, and I nodded even though she couldn't see me.

"I think so. But I'm afraid to try anything in case they linked the computer to the phone, and you have to have both to boot it up. If I log in, there's a good chance they'll know." A sick feeling flooded my stomach, and I nervously eyed the computer. "The monitor looks old enough not to have a camera, but I'd better just look for physical evidence."

"Brey texted me," Jeni said, momentarily straying from her lesson. "Apparently Lacey is putting on all the airs for Royce. She also says Lacey sounds like she's been sucking on a helium balloon because her voice is so high."

"Nerves," I stated, digging through the desk drawers.

Jeni cleared her throat. "That's what it sounds like. Lacey's used the bathroom three times in half an hour according to the latest text message."

Letting out a soft laugh through my nose, I turned around, surveying Ryan's living room. A saggy couch took up a good part of it, an old TV pressed against the off-white wall. Old western and sci-fi films filled the stand beneath it. The walls were covered with newspaper articles that were all similar, each dealing with matters on quantum physics. Except for the coffee table that sat by the couch, every surface in the room was buried beneath piles of scientific journals. The old rocking chair in the corner was filled with science magazines, and I was forced to watch where I stepped because little bits of paper that had hastily scrawled formulas on them littered the floor.

The kitchen wasn't much better, though its counters were bare of any books. Instead, they were buried under piles of dishes, both clean and dirty. I wrinkled my nose.

"This might have been a waste of time," I told Jeni, giving up on the living room and heading to the bedroom. "This place is …" I paused. "I wouldn't say a pigsty, but more of the mess of a bachelor whose only interest is writing a book that requires thousands of hours of research."

I entered the bedroom, and the floor gave a slight creak beneath me. "And no pictures on the walls. Not even in the bedroom. Just newspaper clippings."

As Jeni started her lesson up again, I searched Ryan's room, not surprised to find it in the same state as the living room. After looking under his mattress, I decided that perhaps I was going about this thing all wrong. Ryan clearly wasn't your average guy, and neither was Royce. If they had something to hide, it would be in an unusual place.

My shoulders started to slump in defeat as I looked around the room until my gaze fell on one of the books on the floor. It was a long shot, but maybe there was something in one of them. Bending, I picked one up and rubbed my hand over the glossy cover. My gloves screeched across the surface. The book probably weighed five pounds, and I sat on the sagging, unmade bed to open it.

I wasn't sure what to look for, or if I would even find anything. Ryan was the type of guy who would store all his info in his head, but I believed the attack that left him in the hospital with more broken bones than a bull rider had been a long time coming. If that was true, hopefully he'd left behind notes of some sort, maybe a reminder to lock or hide something because it wasn't safe.

The first book yielded nothing, and neither did the other twenty scattered across the floor, but it was the one in the middle of the stack under the sink in the bathroom that answered at least one question.

A thin slip of blue paper tucked between the pages was wedged in so tightly I had to give it a few sharp tugs before it came out. It was easy to recognize the spidery handwriting that filled the small space as the same that covered the hundreds of pieces of paper scattered around the apartment.

"Tell Blaze," Ryan had written in red ink. Beneath the words I could make out faint marks of what looked like pencil. I held it up to the light and frowned. Eight numbers, looking almost like the ones for a bank account, except there weren't enough of them. The first five were grouped together and followed by a hyphen, and then the final three numbers came after that.

"Some sort of passcode?" I wondered out loud to myself, my soft words loud in the silence of the bathroom. Turning the paper over, I studied at the small drawing of a book that took up the back of it.

"What'd you find?" Jeni asked, voice sharp, and I realized she'd fallen silent a good ten minutes ago.

"I'm not sure, but I think it's pretty important, and if I'm following everything right, I'm going to find clues in some of the books."

Grabbing the one nearest me, I flipped it open after tucking the paper into my pocket. Hastily, I thumbed through the pages, looking for anything that was out of place, a piece of paper, an underlined word, anything.

I stopped on page fifty-six. The six had been circled then gone over with an eraser, as if Ryan only intended for it to be seen by someone who was looking very hard.

"Get a pen and some paper," I told Jeni. "I'm going to quote some numbers to you. If my guess is correct, there will be eight, with a hyphen after the fifth number."

"Ready," she said a moment later.

I checked the time on the clock above the door. Almost eight thirty.

"Six." I turned the pages again, my eyes searching for the faint shine of paper that's seen an eraser. I squinted. "Nine."

After reaching the end of the book, having found several more numbers, Jeni let out a heavy sigh.

"What?" I asked.

"That was only seven numbers," she said. "We're missing one."

Growling, I turned the book over and rubbed my thumb down its thick spine. I repeated my movement, and the smell of soap and spray-on deodorant assailed me. Turning the book so I could see the spine, I shook my head.

"I found it. I found the eighth number. Ryan put the tiniest scratch under the last digit of the volume number."

Jeni heaved an exasperated sigh that ended in a cough. "This guy is something else," she muttered. "Now if we can just figure out what they mean. Oh, hold on, Brey's texting me."

Searching through more of the books as she replied to Brey, I tried to ignore the sweat that dampened the waistband of my pants and the sleeves of my shirt.

"Lacey and Royce have really hit it off," Jeni informed me. "They're making dessert together."

"Thank you, Lord," I breathed, and Jeni echoed me. "Ready for more?" I asked her a moment later. When she confirmed she was, I read off more numbers.

All in all, I found five books with a complete set of eight circled numbers in them, plus the hyphen. The sixth book I picked up only yielded four numbers and I thought all my work had been a rabbit trail until I realized I was holding volume one. When I grabbed the second in the series, I found the remaining four and the hyphen.

"I think I'm done up here," I whispered to Jeni, getting to my feet and heading for the door.

"I think you're done completely," she replied, tone urgent. "Royce is leaving Lacey's. Get out of there. Forget the shop, we can try again."

Fear quickened my steps, and I almost slipped on a piece of paper, barely catching myself on the back of the couch.

"I'm going!" I hissed. My stomach clenched and my neck itched as sweat-soaked hair stuck to it. "I'm almost out."

Running toward the door, I grabbed my backpack and ran down the stairs as quietly as possible, taking them two at a time. I skittered around the corner of Ryan's building. My heart pounded so quickly and erratically I thought I was going into cardiac arrest, but I kept running until I was at the end of the street.

I peeked around the corner of a building and saw Royce sauntering his way toward the shop. When he disappeared around the other side, I sprinted across the street and down the alley to the back of my shop.

Letting myself in, I tore my clothes off and kicked them under my bed, hopping on one foot as I shoved the other through the leg of a pair of lounge pants. Pulling an oversized T-shirt, I tore the black beanie off my head.

"Misty," Jeni warned at the same time a loud knock came to my back door. "You've got company."

"I know that," I whimpered, raking a brush through my sweaty hair. Sliding a wide headband over, I ran into the bathroom. Splashing water onto my face, I washed away all remnants of dust and worked on removing ink from my hands. Some of the notes in the trash at Ryan's were still damp, and the ink transferred to my hands. I almost took the top layer of my skin off as I scrubbed them with a loofah.

The knock came again, and Stetson's tired voice rang out, "Police! Misty, you home?"

"Just a minute!" I called, hurrying back into my room.

"If he asks, the Bible study ended twenty minutes ago," Jeni said.

I spritzed a heavy amount of lemon perfume on. Going to the kitchen, I grabbed an apple from the bowl of the counter and took a big bite out of it, then set it next to the Bible I'd left open on the breakfast bar. A half empty glass of water sat next to it.

"Gotta go," I told Jeni and pulled the earbud from my ear. I stowed it in a kitchen drawer before making my way to the back door. Taking a deep breath, I reached for the handle.

Stetson stood before me as I opened the door, hazel eyes tired and shadowed in the light of the kitchen that shone into them. Autumn darkness shrouded the rest of him.

"I was in the bathroom," I said apologetically. "What's up?"

"Can I come in?" He moved past me even as he asked.

"I guess so," I replied, shutting the door before following him.

Reaching the breakfast bar, Stetson turned to face me. "Misty, can you tell me what you were up to this evening for say, the last two and a half hours?"

I struggled to meet his eyes. "I was having a Bible study with Jeni." Making a show of looking at the stove clock, I widened my eyes in innocence. "It ended about twenty minutes ago. Why? Did something else happen?"

Stetson let out a heavy sigh and I studied him, getting a strong whiff of smoke as I took a step closer. Though he'd obviously washed up since coming back from Jamie's, there was still specks of ash in his dark hair and a line of black soot went down his neck.

Clenching my hands into fists as my sides, I struggled with the urge to wipe the soot away.

"Royce just called to let me know someone broke into Ryan's apartment while he was having dinner with Lacey." Tone holding a note of fatigue, Stetson's face was haggard. Shoulders slightly slumped as if his back hurt, he stared at me. "Did you see anything? Hear anything?"

Clearing my throat, I gestured toward the Bible on the counter. "No, sorry. I was pretty wrapped up in that study."

Eyeing the tall cowboy in front of me, concern flooded me. "Stetson, you look tired. Do you want to do this tomorrow?"

Letting out a loud exhale, he shrugged his shoulders. "Probably," he mumbled, and I noticed the hoarseness in his voice. "I'm too beat to try to figure this out right now." The wheezing cough he let out propelled me forward.

Touching a hand to his forearm I said, "Are you okay? Do you need to see Jeff?"

Stetson shook his head, the corners of his mouth tight. "Nah, he already checked me. I inhaled a lot of smoke today, but I'll be fine. I just need some rest. I'm gonna let Chase handle this one and do the rest in the morning."

I dropped my hand away from his arm. "So, why'd you stop over?"

"Firstly," he replied over his shoulder, "to make sure you were okay. Secondly, to figure out what you had to do with it." He reached for the door handle. "But I think I'd better leave that for tomorrow."

"What about Ryan?" I asked, darting forward. "Did Terri call you yet?"

Stetson turned and gazed down at me with weary eyes, and I silently prayed that Blaze would hurry and come back.

"Misty, Ryan passed away about twenty minutes ago. The swelling in his brain was just too much, and they couldn't save him. I'm sorry."

I pressed my hands against my mouth, and tears filled my eyes. "Not Ryan," I whispered. "That poor man. He had so many plans for his life. Oh, Stetson, his poor family!"

Shoulders sagging, Stetson looked down. "Yeah. I was really praying he'd pull through, and it looked like he would but then ..." Voice trailing off, he coughed.

"Were the doctors able to find out anything? Did he say anything before he passed?" I asked, crossing my arms over my chest.

"Look, Misty, I get you wanna know what's going on with the case, but can this wait until tomorrow? This is a murder now, and that changes everything. So, maybe we could talk over lunch after church?"

I blinked at the suggestion and the reminder that it was almost Sunday.

"Esposito's?" I asked. The small Italian restaurant was much more private with its small booths than Aubrey's wide-open diner.

Stetson gave a nod and turned back toward the door. "I think that'll work. And you'd better have a believable explanation as to what you were doing tonight while someone broke into Ryan's apartment."

I locked up after him and headed back to the kitchen. After drinking a glass of water, I debated on what to wear the next morning. Usually I went with whichever maxi dress was closest to the front of my closet, but if I was going out with Stetson ... I shook the pesky thought away. "This isn't a date, Misty," I told myself firmly. "This is business, and unless you want to wind up spending Thanksgiving in a jail cell, you'd better be on your toes tomorrow!"

Turning out the kitchen lights, I made my way to my bedroom. I stared into my small closet and rubbed my chin. On second thought, maybe I should go ahead and fancy up a bit. It didn't escape me that Stetson was attracted to me, and while I didn't for a moment think looking pretty would deter him from his job, I hoped it would make it harder for him to slap cuffs on me.

I grabbed one of my fanciest dresses and hung it over my bathroom door. Its shimmering purples, blues, and pinks would look great with my hair, and I owned the perfect pair of sandals to go with it. Best of all, it didn't require ironing, so I could sleep to the last minute. My hair never took long, even if I decided to go with a more complex style than my usual chignon.

Slipping into bed, I opened my emails on my phone, reading the one Jeni sent me and memorized the main points of the study she had taught me while I'd done some less-than-godly things. Once I was confident enough in what I'd retained to tell Stetson over lunch, I closed the app.

I plugged my phone in to charge before turning off my lamp and settled back onto my pillow. As I stared up at my ceiling, the soft whir of a fan running on low in the corner a soothing white noise, my mind strayed back to the numbers I'd found in the books in Ryan's apartment. Jeni tried Googling what they might mean but came up empty. I wondered if I should give them to Stetson, who might have better luck.

Turning on my side, I wished Aubrey was in town. She had a head for puzzles, and, in my opinion, was the braver of the two of us. And she had the ear of a policeman. Hands under my cheek, I stared at the wall.

For a long moment, I debated telling Stetson about what I'd found, but finally, I decided not to, unwilling to face his wrath. I could only hope and pray it wouldn't turn out to be a mistake.

7

"Great message!" Jesse told Pastor Brent the next morning, shaking his hand.

"Yes," Suzanne, Brent's wife added as she came to stand by her husband. "Preaching on how no matter the size of the sin, all are deadly and lead to the same destination."

"I tend to think some sins are a necessary evil," Seth said as he moved past me. "Some of us are just born to do bad things and never see redemption, and that's just how it is."

Staring after him as he left, I wondered about the bitterness that colored his tone but was distracted by Brent extending his hand to me. Swallowing hard, I took it, my own hand sweaty from the conviction of his message.

"Good service, Pastor," I told him, and before he could reply, I beat a quick path to the door, afraid that if I stuck around any longer, he'd be able to read the abject guilt on my face. As it was, I was certain the Holy Spirit had told on me, for Brent seemed to stare at me for much of his fiery sermon.

In such a hurry to leave, I almost knocked down Flamingo Springs' newest resident, Abigail Richards, owner of the toy store. Brent made sure to welcome her from the pulpit that morning, and she seemed like a kind woman, the clip holding her blond hair away from her face matching her earrings.

"I'm so sorry," I apologized, grabbing her arm to steady her.

The smile she gave me was big, and the scent of her light perfume surrounded me.

"No problem," she said softly. Her eyes, the color of denim, sparkled. I noticed her hands were slender. The nails were dotted with what looked like paint, and her forearm had small green stains on it, as if she'd been undertaking some home improvement projects. Or decorating a toy store.

I opened my mouth to introduce myself but was interrupted when Suzanne pulled her away from me and invited her to dinner. I continued to the door. Though our encounter lasted less than twenty seconds, I found myself moving her onto the innocent side of the list of names I'd written down the night before. There was a goodness in her eyes, and I felt certain she was exactly what she was presenting—a young businesswoman opening her first store.

Marie agreed to let Stetson and me in an hour early to talk, and I pondered the points from Brent's message as I made my way to Esposito's.

My heel caught on the boardwalk. I tripped and almost fell against the large window that took up much of the front of restaurant, regretting my decision to wear wedges. After steadying myself, I reached for the handle on the frosted glass door and entered Vincent and Marie's pride and joy. The warm wind pushed against my back.

The smell of garlic filled the air, and I allowed my eyes to adjust to the dimness of the cozy eatery before moving forward. Soft Italian jazz reached my ears about the same time that Stetson's voice called my name. Turning, I spotted him seated in the corner booth across the room, dressed in his usual apparel of boots, jeans, and his tan dress shirt.

Face flushing, I hurried toward him, almost falling on the table as my left heel caught on the carpet.

"What are you thinking?" I hissed at him as I fell gracelessly into the seat across from him. "Picking the 'Proposal Booth'? Are you nuts?"

I glared at him while I rubbed my throbbing foot. The 'Proposal Booth' was the area of Esposito's diners requested to sit when planning to propose. Tucked into a corner, it was the only booth that had curtains around it, and I could almost hear the wheels in Marie's head turning as she took our drink order, a soda for Stetson and iced tea for me.

Stetson chuckled. "Relax. We're leaving the curtains open." He brushed a hand through his dark hair and placed his hat on the black leather seat beside him. "It's just lunch. And if people wanna argue, well, not much I can do about that." The booth gave a slight creak as he settled back, the toe of his boot nudging my shoe as he situated his long legs.

"Spill it," he drawled. "I wanna have this over with before Marie brings my steak."

Lines of innocence rehearsed, I wet my lips, but before I could get the first word out, Stetson held up a hand.

"But let me just say," he met my eyes and winked, "you look great."

If his intention was to fluster me, he succeeded. It took two dry coughs and a round of rearranging my silverware roll before I could reply. The dim lantern above the table cast shadows as it swayed in front of an AC vent.

"Are you feeling better today?" I finally got out, deciding to ignore his compliment, not sure I wanted to step into those waters. "You look like you got some sleep."

Stetson nodded. A strand of hair fell across his tanned

forehead, and my eyes were drawn to his throat as he swallowed. Wishing he'd chosen a booth by a window, I had nowhere to look but at him. Sure, I could have turned and stared at the wall and pretended it was a window, but I was already in trouble for toeing the line with the law. I didn't need my sanity questioned on top of that.

"I did," he said, pausing to thank Marie as she set our glasses down on the glossy wooden table. The sounds of Vincent rattling around in the kitchen reached our booth, and she smiled as she took our order. Steak for Stetson, and shrimp fettuccine for me, with a shared dish of spicy mozzarella bites.

"After I took some allergy medicine to combat the stuffy nose from all the smoke I inhaled, I felt brand new." Stetson pinned me with a look as he took a sip of his soda. "Royce was pretty hyped up about last night, but I think he understood there wasn't a whole lot I could do beside securing the scene and checking for prints."

"About that," I said, opening the straw Marie placed next to my sweaty glass, "I really didn't hear a thing. I was kinda busy with the Bible study Jeni was giving me." Taking a pull of my own beverage, the taste of lemon and tea refreshed my suddenly dry throat. "Do you think I should be worried about someone trying to break in? Or should Brey, since she's working at the bakery on her own while Aubrey's gone?"

Stetson pushed his glass away. "I really don't think so," he said, crossing his arms on the top of the table. "Whoever did it used a crowbar to break the door jam, but it doesn't look like they got very far. Hardly anything was disturbed, and I couldn't find any prints." Pausing, he wiped the water ring from his glass around the table. "The perp wasn't very bright, I don't think."

Choking on the sip of tea I'd just taken, I squirmed under Stetson's stern gaze. "What makes you say that?" I managed to get out, eyes watering as I fought the urge to cough.

"If they'd just looked, they would have found the door was unlocked," Stetson explained, hazel eyes so narrow they were almost slits as he watched me. "Royce said he lost the key to it the other day somewhere between here and Houston and just hadn't gotten around to getting a new one yet. Small town like this, he didn't think it would be a problem to leave the door unlocked for a night or two."

Mimicking Stetson, I crossed my arms, then quickly lowered them, letting one elbow rest on the table and placing my free hand in my lap.

"Dumb perp indeed," I agreed with Stetson. "But I guess that's why they've taken to breaking into places."

Stetson eyed me, lips parted as if he was one breath away from coming out and saying he knew I was the criminal. Before he could speak, an angry voice interrupted us.

"So, this is what you meant by investigating the break-in," Royce snarled down at us, hands curled into fists as they hung at his sides. "Taking your girlfriend out for lunch instead of trying to figure out who murdered my brother!" He snorted. "You cops are all alike. All lies and fakery."

"Excuse me," Stetson said, not twitching as he stared up at Royce, whose wrinkled khaki shorts and paint-stained polo shirt smelled of latex. "You're interrupting a possible witness statement. If you want to discuss the case, I'll be in the office at four."

Royce pointed a finger at me. "Witness? More like criminal! You and I both know this blue-headed busybody is the one who broke in, and I wouldn't doubt she had something to do with Ryan's death." Hand shaking, he stepped closer, but before I could move, Stetson was on his feet. Royce pulled back.

"Now look here," Stetson growled. "You two may have gotten off on the wrong foot, but Misty was a good friend of

Ryan, and she's been a great help with the case. She's also one of the only people who would have been able to see something last night, so, if you don't mind, I'd like to hear about that."

"Well, I ..." Royce sputtered.

But Stetson wasn't finished, and tearing my gaze away from the two, I saw Vincent and Marie poke their heads into the dining area from the open doorway of the kitchen. Marie held a platter to her side while Vincent brandished a large pair of tongs that he clacked together. The sound was loud in the quiet restaurant.

"And another thing," Stetson continued. "Let's not forget that I was at your brother's place until almost two in the morning securing everything and getting you a room to stay in at the hotel, courtesy of the county. After that, I had to go back to my office and file the report, and this is after I helped put out a brush fire earlier that afternoon. I'm also filling in as acting sheriff."

Stetson leaned forward, and I took the moment to admire his strong shoulders. The edge of the tattoo that wrapped around his upper bicep peeked out from under his sleeve. "Do you know what time it was when I finally clocked out and went home?"

When Royce mumbled something in reply.

Stetson let out a laugh. "That's right, it was late. Real late. As in, almost five in the morning. I worked almost twenty-four hours straight, so I feel that I'm entitled to take at least eight off before I clock back in."

Turning, he made a show of checking the clock on the wall across the room. "It's barely twelve thirty, and I'm already back at work attempting to interview someone, because whether you believe it or not, I care about this case, and I want people brought to justice."

He leaned forward a few more inches and glared down at

Royce until the artist flinched, one arm covering his stomach in a protective gesture. "If you want to help me figure out what's going on, you'll stop dogging my every step and let me do my job."

Mumbling an apology, Royce turned and ran from the restaurant, almost tripping in his flipflops. Once the door swung shut behind him and Vincent and Marie finished applauding my shining deputy in jeans, Stetson sat back down, his mouth a thin line. Before I could say a word, he pinned me to my seat with a glare, and his dimples were slashes in his cheeks.

"I swear, Misty, you better be innocent in all of this because I just chewed that boy out on the pretense that you are."

I leaned back from the table so that Marie could set our plates of food down, "I already told you I was with Jeni." I took a deep inhale of the delicious scent wafting up from my steaming plate of shrimp and noodles. "No matter how many times you ask me what I was doing last night, no matter how many different ways you phrase it, my answer is going to be the same."

Taking a sip from my glass, I settled back into the booth, staring at the man who sat across from me. "Before we continue this, would you mind saying grace?"

Tan forehead wrinkled in frustration, Stetson gave a curt nod and bowed his head. I followed suit, silently praying that God would somehow transport me out of the booth and into the next county.

"Lord," Stetson said. "We thank You for this day and this time of, er, fellowship." My lips twitched even as I bowed my own head, eyes closed. "And we thank You for this food and ask that You bless it and bless our time together. In Jesus' name, amen."

Echoing the last part, I raised my head, and above the

delectable smells of garlic mixing with the smoky tones of Stetson's steak, I could smell his aftershave. The intriguing scent gave me a pause as I reached for my silverware.

Stetson looked at me as he did the same, a gleam in his eyes. But before he could pin me down again, I spoke, skittering, quite literally, away from being found out.

"Did Ryan say anything at all to the doctors?" I asked, forking up a bite of noodles dripping in creamy sauce. "I'm sure Brey will be glad when Terri gets back."

Stetson sliced a bite of steak before answering, forearms rippling with his motions. "He kept asking for his mother and refused to say anything about what happened. Said he couldn't remember. He passed away not long after that."

"I thought he would want to talk," I said, patting my lips with the white cloth napkin my silverware had been rolled in. "You said that last part like you don't believe it. You think he was lying, don't you?"

Stetson shrugged, taking a chug of his soda. "Call it a gut feeling, but yeah, I do. The only other thing he said was to have me collect all the books from his apartment. That was the very last thing he said before he slipped into a coma. The doctors told me his girlfriend kept cutting him off when he'd speak, so even if he wanted to say more, he couldn't."

"Did they think she really was his girlfriend?" I asked. "I mean, Ryan has never once mentioned a girlfriend to anyone here, and he never left town, and never had any visitors."

Tucking his bite of baked potato into his cheek, Stetson gave me a smirk. "Jealous, are we?" he teased.

I flushed, shaking my head. "Come on, Stetson, you know as well as I do that this whole thing reeks. Are you going to take the books?"

Taking a bite of shrimp, I shivered as the AC swirled cool air around us. If Ryan wanted Stetson to have his books, he must have wanted for Stetson to see the strange codes he'd put in them.

"Soon as I'm done here, I'll go grab them," Stetson assured me. Nose twitching, he sniffed the air. "Do you smell that?" he asked, slightly turning toward the outside of the booth. "Smells like smoke."

Shaking my head, I could only smell our food and started to say as much but was cut off when Vincent popped out of the kitchen, wiping his hands on his apron. "Where's the fire?" he asked. Stetson tossed his napkin down on the table.

"That's what I'm about to find out," he said grimly, sliding out from the booth.

Doing the same, I hobbled along after him in my wedges, the sparkly straps digging into my ankles as I struggled to keep up. Vincent opened the front door and stepped outside. The smell of smoke quickly surrounded us.

"That smells like paper burning," I commented, and looking down the street as he stepped out onto the sidewalk, Stetson grunted.

"Something tells me you're right about that," he muttered, and moving out next to him, I watched as Royce jogged down the street toward us. Thin plumes of smoke curled out the windows of Ryan's apartment. Royce had streaks of black down his arms and across his face, and a good portion of his right pant leg was charred.

"It's out," he called, cheeks bright red as he came to a stop in front us, chest heaving. Someone pressed a bottle of water into his hand. A small crowd had gathered around him as store owners poured out from their respective homes.

Abigail Richards, owner of the soon-coming toy store, stood away from the crowd, her face twisted into a frown. Ratty jeans streaked with paint, the brush she held dripped more of it to the dirt street, and I could almost guess what she was thinking.

Flamingo Springs might not have been the best place to open a children's store.

Clear eyes met mine and she lifted an eyebrow, but I could only send her a weak smile. What else could I do when whispers of murder were going through the crowd as people speculated if what happened Ryan would happen to his brother.

Royce took a swig from the bottle, his dark hair tousled and covered in white specks. "That'll teach me to try to cook."

"What happened?" Stetson asked quietly.

From my place slightly behind him I watched his shoulders tense, clearly not believing anything Royce was saying.

"I tried to cook up some chicken, and the grease caught fire," Royce said, making a face.

Studying him, I could almost believe him. Almost. Until his eyes darted to the left. "It splattered onto the counter and caught fire to the books Ryan left stacked there."

Shoulders drooping, he gave us a dejected look, and Lacey moved forward to wrap a comforting arm around his shoulders. She'd been just as worried as me when Stetson ordered me to meet him for lunch, concerned about the charges she might face if he found out her part in keeping Royce busy while I broke into his brother's apartment. More than once as she'd prayed next to me in church, I'd heard her specifically ask the Lord to have Stetson go easy on her.

Now, as she stood next to my lead suspect, playing the part of being a concerned friend, I fought the urge to pull her away from him. Royce was lying. I had been in Ryan's apartment the night before and there hadn't been a single book in the kitchen. Why he wanted to burn them in the first place was beyond me. Why not just throw them out? If he wanted to hide the codes hidden in them, why not do it in a quiet way instead of drawing everyone's attention?

"But don't worry," Royce said.

From the corner of my eye I saw Stetson's jaw clench.

"I got everything put out. Ryan's probably gonna kill me when he finds out." Pausing, Royce looked down, voice thickening with tears. "Except now he never will."

"Books are replaceable," Marie said from behind me. "You aren't. We're so glad you're okay."

Royce winced and gestured toward his leg. "Except for my leg. I think I burnt it a bit trying to put everything out." The smile he gave Marie was wide as he played the part of the hero, but his eyes were dark.

"Come to the church with me and Suzanne," Brent told him, still dressed in his suit. "Jeff is out of town today, but I used to be a paramedic back in the day, so I can fix you up." Nodding at Suzanne, they led Royce and Lacey down the street, the crowd dispersing as they did so, murmuring about what a tragedy it was.

"Wait for me!" a raspy voice called, and turning, I watched as Seth scurried down the street, white hair catching in the sun.

"Royce, are you okay?" he said when he finally reached the trio.

Pastor Brent tried not to be too obvious about keeping Royce's sooty leg from brushing against his slacks.

Royce sent Seth a weak grin. "I will be," he said. "You can come with, though, and hear what happened."

Grabbing his arm as they walked, Seth whispered in his ear, shaking the young man. Pulling away from him, Royce glared down at him and said something, but I couldn't make out what. Feeling my gaze, the two looked at me. Royce's face was sullen while Seth gave me a smile that seemed too bright. I wondered what I missing.

The group moved toward the church, out of ear shot. I stepped forward so that I stood directly next to Stetson. "Shall we finish lunch?" I asked, a bit queasy as I realized that Royce was doing everything he could to gain the townspeople's sympathy.

Stetson shook his head. "I think I've lost my appetite," he said, and after Marie and Vincent disappeared back inside the restaurant to box our leftovers up, he turned to me.

"Now would be a good time to tell me what was in those books."

I stared up at him, wide eyed.

"What are you talking about?" I asked, doing my best to sound confused.

Stetson grabbed my shoulders, holding me still when I tried to turn away. "Oh, no," he said. "You aren't going anywhere. Not until you tell me what you found."

"I told you I'm innocent," I exclaimed, trying to squirm away from him, fearful that the entire town was watching what looked like a lovers' quarrel. "I was having a Bible study!"

"I get that," Stetson snorted, tightening his grip as he stared into my eyes. "But you've never said where you were when you were having that study. And for that matter, when I talked to Jeni, she danced around that answer too. So, tell me, Misty, where were you while you had your Bible study last night?"

Stilling beneath the strong hands that gripped my shoulders, I met Stetson's eyes. "I was at Ryan's. I'm the one who broke in. There. I admitted it. Now you can arrest me."

Stetson gave a low laugh, eyes dancing in the sunlight that shone into them. "Darlin'," he drawled, "if I was gonna arrest you, I would have done it last night while you were doing your snooping."

Releasing me, he put some distance between us, tucking his fingers into his back pockets as he rocked back on his heels. A slow grin stretched his lips as he watched pink creep up my neck and spread to my cheeks. With my blue hair and red face,

I probably looked like I was trying to mimic the American flag, and it took all I had not to stomp my foot.

Holding my tongue, I thanked Marie as she handed me my to-go container, but as soon as she disappeared back inside her business and the door swung shut behind her, I let loose, and I'm not too sure that I *didn't* stomp my foot.

"Do you ever get tired of playing this cat-and-mouse game, Stetson?" I demanded, voice sharp, throat burning as I struggled to control myself. "Does it empower you when time and time again you make me feel stupid? When you belittle me? When you smirk at me and insinuate that you're tolerating me like I'm a child?"

The hem of my dress fluttered in the quick breeze that swirled around us, stirring up sand in the street. The wind chimes Jesse had placed outside the front of his store the day before sent clear soprano notes through the air as they clanged together. A piece of grit lodged itself in the corner of my mouth, and I licked my lips. The dirt scraped across my teeth.

Confrontations in movies are often glamorous, an edge of your seat experience where romantic tension cracks through the air, and the words flung between the two parties are eloquent, dramatically spoken. But it's not like that.

Sweat pooled at my lower back, and I felt anything but glamorous. Lunch sat heavy in my stomach, and my mouth was dry. Eyes burning, I stared at Stetson, saw the small freckle on his left ear, took in the way his mouth thinned as I spoke, watched his shoulders hunch forward a bit as he held his to-go box.

"I'm not a child, Stetson," I said softly. "I'm someone who cares about the people of this town. These are my friends, my family. It's fine if you don't like my snooping, and I admit that what I did last night was not only illegal, it was immoral, but you know what? Punish me for it. Confront me about it. Confront me about the things I do that bother you. But don't patronize me. Don't tolerate me like I'm a little girl who's taken a fancy for ponies when last week my interest was ballet. Don't do that to me."

The container in my hand squeaked as I shifted, and I dropped my gaze. "I'm sorry this turned out to be such a miserable lunch. Send me a bill, and I'll be sure to pay for my half."

Stepping down onto the street, I was very aware of how silent the deputy had been my entire tirade, how he never once even opened his mouth to refute my accusations. "When and if you're ready to talk to me like I'm an adult, you know where I am."

I walked away from him and heard his boots scrape as he started to follow me, then stopped. I knew Marie and Vincent were still glued to the front window. My words may have been quiet, but they were also powerful and honest.

Though my heart felt like it was about to start bleeding any moment, as no one likes to be treated like a child when they most certainly aren't one, not for one second did I consider giving up my pursuit of finding out what really happened to Ryan. In fact, he was the very thing I discussed that night when I met with Lacey, Brey, and Jeni at Aubrey's for an evening snack.

"I've Googled and web searched what those numbers could mean, but I've got nothing," Jeni said over her plate of pancakes.

"I could ask one of my lawyer friends," Lacey said, wrapping her hands around a tall tumbler of iced tea, "but I think he'd get suspicious."

Nodding, I took a bite of the syrup drizzled pancake Brey insisted I eat, and looking down at the blue plate, I let out a surprised cough.

Brey looked across the table at me, an almost mischievous grin on her face. "Good, aren't they?" Her slim frame gave no indication of how many sweets she ate a day, and she looked sleepy despite the cup of coffee she held.

"Is this espresso?" I asked her, momentarily distracted from the case.

Grinning, she gave a slight nod as Lacey reached over and took my fork, stabbing a bite of the sweet breakfast food and shoving it into her mouth.

"Yup," Brey said. "Aubrey has been working with a vendor up in Wisconsin who owns a maple syrup farm and likes to experiment around with different flavors. This is their newest one—espresso maple. We just got the shipment in yesterday, and you guys are the first to taste it. Aubrey thinks it'll be a hit. I think she's right, don't you?"

After a chorus of "Yes!" filled the room, I settled back in my chair with a deep sigh. Lacey sent me a concerned look. Pale hair draped over one shoulder in a messy fishtail braid, she fiddled with the loose ends of it, her bright pink shirt making her tan skin glow.

"Thinking about Ryan?" she asked quietly, and I nodded, meeting her gray gaze.

"Yeah," I admitted as Brey drained her coffee cup. "We found those sequences, and at first, I thought it was just something Ryan was working on. But hearing how the last thing he said was to make sure the doctors told Stetson to get his books tells me they must be important."

"And then Royce oh-so-accidentally had that fire today," Jeni interjected, the soft yellow light of the fixture above us lending a copper hue to her bright red hair. "He deliberately burned them."

"Right," I agreed. "And I can't help but go back to how Stetson said Ryan's girlfriend kept hushing him."

"I think she heard him tell the doctors about the books. Brey's voice was serious. "That's the only thing that could make sense. Whatever those numbers mean, it's important. You need to tell Stetson."

"We need to investigate the girlfriend," Lacey said. "Firstly, I don't think Ryan really had one, and secondly, unless we find something out, the case is pretty much closed. Either he didn't talk to protect himself, or he did it to protect someone else."

"Gotta be someone else." I leaned forward and rested my forearms on the table after shoving my hair behind my ears. "If he was doing it to protect himself, wouldn't he know whoever tried to kill him the first time would try again as soon as he got out of the hospital and didn't have a guard anymore?"

"I agree," Jeni said. Fingers flying as she took notes on her phone, she bit her lip, then finally looked up. "I think we need to find out who that girlfriend is and see if we can figure out her angle." Cutting the last word off, she came to an abrupt end.

I raised an eyebrow. "And?" I prompted, my voice dry, knowing what was coming.

"And," Jeni sighed, looking away from me, "I think you need to give Stetson the numbers. If you don't, not only are you considered to be withholding information that could further an ongoing case, you're also slowing us down."

"I'll think about it," I said after a long moment. Brey and Lacey busied themselves, trying not to impose on the sore subject of one ornery deputy. I looked at Lacey. "You never really said how your dinner with Royce went."

Lacey winced. "I mean, it was okay, but the guy is weird. Sweet, but weird."

"How so?" Brey asked, scratching her jaw as Jeni pulled her phone out again. "Like, creepy weird? Awkward weird?"

Lacey lifted a shoulder, wrinkling her nose. "Neither. Weird in a way like he thought he was being watched. Like he was afraid that at any moment the door was going to be busted down and the cops were gonna raid us."

"Guilty conscience," I guessed. "Whatever is going on, that guy is right in the middle of it."

"I think the same," Jeni agreed. "It's just figuring out how to prove it."

"I still think that toy store owner is in on it," Brey said, frowning. "I mean, she just shows up from nowhere, doesn't know a soul, and starts a business."

"I don't think she is," I replied, tracing my fork through the sticky crumbs left on my plate. "When I talked to her this morning at church, I didn't get that kind of vibe from her. She seemed really nice. A gentle soul, as they say."

Lacey nodded. "That's what I noticed too. She didn't say much to me, but she was extremely sweet."

"Being sweet could be a front," Brey warned, then weakening, added, "but she does seem nice."

"We'll keep her on the list," Jeni decided. "It won't hurt to keep an eye on her."

After another hour of deliberating over the case, we decided to call it a night, each of us having an early morning the next day as we were cramming in as much work as possible before Thursday, which would be Thanksgiving Day.

Lacey had back-to-back appointments at her salon up until Wednesday afternoon, when she would leave for Houston. Brey would be busy at the diner until she left with Lacey, who would drop her at the airport so she could catch her flight to Los Angeles to spend the holiday with Kasey, and Jeni would be driving over to Galveston.

Of the four of us, I was the only one who wasn't going anywhere. Holidays were the time of year my parents took their cruises and extravagant trips around the world. As I crossed the street to my store, I kicked at the ground.

This case was frustrating, and a lot more difficult than I'd thought it would be. It was as if we were spinning our wheels, getting nowhere, and I was ready to give up. But every time I let the thought of giving in flit through my mind, I would see Ryan's still form in the back alley, his blood drenching the earth, and I knew I had to keep pushing.

Reaching the front door of my studio, I stopped. Warmth filled me. A small vase sat on the sidewalk, filled with wildflowers that looked to have come from Jesse's grocery mart. A small envelope was taped to the side of the vase. I stooped down and picked them up. Unlocking the door, I made my way to the kitchen where I set the vase on the breakfast bar. Opening the envelope, I was greeted with Stetson's bold handwriting scrawled across the small piece of stock paper.

"I'm sorry," it read. "Can we start over?"

Setting the note down, I leaned forward to sniff one of the flowers, a purple daisy with glitter on its petals.

"I think that can be arranged," I murmured to myself with a smile. Stetson wasn't the only who needed to apologize, though, and I knew that first thing in the morning, I was going to make things right between us.

After pulling on loose sweatpants and an old hoodie, I made my way to the kitchen, hopped up on one of the stools at the breakfast bar, and turned on my laptop. The next few hours were spent answering comments on my YouTube channel and replying to numerous emails, my headphones plugged into the side of the thin computer, music pulsing in my ears.

Once I'd accomplished as much as I could work-wise, I logged onto Facebook, once again turning to the profile of the woman who claimed to be Ryan's girlfriend—Cynthia. Her beaming smile struck me just as it had the first time, as did the happiness in her eyes. I studied her, wondered who she was, where she spent her free time when she wasn't working at the zoo. Scouring her page, I once more came up with nothing, and I released a loud sigh.

After forty-five minutes of getting nowhere on social media, I tried looking up what the numbers I'd found might mean. After countless attempts of entering the info into my search bar I finally sat back and admitted defeat, at least for the moment. Staring at the screen of my laptop, its backlight set to night mode, I stretched an arm out and pecked at the numbers on my keypad. Entering five numbers, then a hyphen, then three more numbers, I hit the enter key.

My eyes widened as the search results filled my screen, I leaned forward, the crescendo of a violin solo filling my ears as I stared at the results. Icy hot pricks raced down my arms, and a shudder went through me as I realized what I'd just stumbled on.

So focused on the info displayed on the screen in front of me, I didn't know anyone had entered my home until something dropped past my face and wrapped around my neck. Reaching up, I found a rope to be the culprit. It bit into my skin as my attacker tightened it and dragged me off the barstool to the floor, where I landed with a crash. My legs tangled in the rungs of the stool. My laptop hit the floor, tearing my earbuds from my ears as it did so. Fingernails scraped on the flooring as I was dragged backward. My vision blacked out at the edges. Fire ate at my throat as blood pounded in my ears.

Panic filled me, and after a brief second of struggling, my karate training kicked in. A moment later, my attacker lay on the floor in a fetal position, clutching his nether region. He groaned about his face, which dripped blood onto my clean flooring through the black ski mask he wore.

Stepping back to grab my phone and call Stetson, I was met with a wall of flesh, and turning, I found myself facing another masked man. It wasn't long before he, too, was laid out on the floor, but in the time that it took me to overcome him, the first man gained his bearings. When I turned to make sure he was still down, something hard connected with the side of my head, and I dropped to the floor.

Landing in a twisted position, the breath whooshed from my lungs, but I felt nothing. No pain from the wound on my head, nor from my hip, which took the brunt of my fall. I tried to open my eyes but couldn't. There was no sensation in my hands as I attempted to curl my fingers, and I barely felt the impact of someone's foot connecting with my back. I could only lay on the floor of my home and listen as my home was ransacked, hear the shatter of my laptop as it was stomped on, the heavy crash of the vase of flowers from Stetson being thrown against a wall, the smell of cigarette smoke overwhelming my senses. Not knowing what was going to happen to me, the only thing I could do was listen and silently pray.

The minutes crept by as my attackers continued to destroy my home. After a while, I managed to open my eyes a tiny bit, but they slammed shut again when someone grabbed a handful of my hair and jerked my head up.

"Take this as a warning," a man growled into my ear, his breath smelling of cigarettes. "Stop snooping. Keep it up, and next time you'll get more than a bump on the head." Releasing my hair, he let my head drop back to the floor. Glass crunched under his feet as he left. The door opened, then closed. And then it was silent.

Forcing my eyes open, I was met with the sight of a

completely trashed home. Feeling slowing crept back into my body as I dragged myself to the kitchen, wincing when I cut my thigh on a shard of glass from a plate that was shattered on the floor, a plate that only an hour earlier had been drying in a metal rack in the sink. Sobs shook my body as I used cabinet handles to pull myself up against the counter.

Vision narrow, my breath came out in gasps, and my back ached. It took me two tries before I was able to reach out and grab the handset phone that sat by the toaster. My cell phone lay in pieces next to my laptop.

I dialed the only number that would come to mind. Sliding back down to the floor, I shook as I looked around at my small home. Many of my cabinet doors were ripped off their hinges, and most of my dishes were broken. Knives had been used to carve deep grooves in my walls and countertops, and I dreaded what I knew my personal quarters must look like.

When Stetson finally answered his phone, his voice groggy, I couldn't speak. When he said my name, sounding more awake, the only thing I could do was sob.

8

Brey was the first to arrive at my home, a butcher knife in one hand, pepper spray in the other as she ran through the back door. Seth was right behind her, bringing up the rear, holding a pistol at his side.

"I told you to let me go first!" he half shouted at Brey.

She ignored him and fell to her knees next to me, knife clattering to the floor. Hair in a tangled knot on the top of her head, her lounge pants were inside out, but her hands were strong and gentle as she pressed a dish cloth to the side of my head, her lifeguard training from high school kicking in.

"Misty, can you hear me?"

I stared at her blearily while Seth moved past us to scout out my home, his gun now pointed in front of him.

"Yeah," I finally muttered. "Brey, I don't feel so good."

She shook her head, bun drooping to one side. The dim light of the kitchen chandelier reflected a pale spot in her worried eyes. "I can see why."

Her cold fingers pressed against my neck, feeling my pulse, her other hand still applying pressure to my head, which, I discovered only moments before, was oozing blood everywhere and had left a trail when I crawled to the phone.

"Isn't Aubrey the one who is supposed to get hit upside the head?" she joked.

I tried to grin but instead began crying again.

"Jeff is on his way," she told me.

Seth, now back in the room and adjusting his robe, set his pistol on the counter. "No one here," he said just as Lacey burst through the back door, brandishing a cast iron skillet.

Not sure if I was hallucinating or not, I stared at her.

She must have noticed my confused gaze. "Don't even start," she said. Brey held back a laugh while Seth snorted.

Lacey is one of the fanciest people I know, so I expected her nightwear to be just as beautiful and over the top as her clothes, but instead of a silk nightie, she was clothed in worn-out house slippers, a polka dot housecoat my grandma would have loved, and cold cream.

Platinum hair bound up in rag curlers, anti-snore strip across her nose, an earplug hung halfway out of one ear. It fell to the floor as she dropped down next to me. The skillet lay in her lap as she took over applying pressure to my head.

"Are you hurt anywhere else?" Brey asked.

I leaned close to Lacey, the scent of cold cream, and sore muscle patches a homey smell that made me feel a bit more grounded. "My back," I finally said. The room started to spin again. Seth went to the back door, standing guard, and I heard him talking on his phone, presumably to Stetson.

"They kicked me in the back," I said. "I don't know how hard—I couldn't feel anything for a while after they hit my head."

Eyes squinted, I looked up at Brey from my position against Lacey's chest. "I had just found something on my laptop when they broke in, but I can't remember what it was. I can't remember what I was looking for or what I was doing besides being on my laptop." I glanced toward the place my phone and computer were now little more than sparkly dust. "And from the looks of it, I won't be finding out either."

"Let's not worry about that right now," Brey soothed me. "You have a concussion. The last thing you need is to get more agitated."

We waited in silence after that, and the minutes passed slowly. Jeff was coming in from out of town, so Brey and Lacey did what they could to make me comfortable without moving me. Everyone heard Stetson before we saw him, his truck sliding across the gravel in the alley behind my building, gears grinding as he threw it into park.

"About time you answered," he barked into his phone, most likely at Chase. "We've got a break in and assault at Misty's. Get down here. Now!"

Slipping his phone into his pocket, he knelt next to me, digging through the First Aid bag he was carrying. Face drawn, lines fanned out from his mouth, and his hair was completely flat on one side. A red mark from what looked like the corner of a pillow went across one cheek. Green shirt on backwards, his pants were zipped but not buttoned, and scruff covered his jaw, but he was the most beautiful sight I'd ever seen. Before he could say anything, I started sobbing again.

Up until that moment I hadn't felt safe, and now that I did, I was overwhelmed.

"Oh God," Lacey prayed under her breath, "Oh God, we don't know what happened, but we know that You are in control. Father, comfort Misty right now, strengthen her. Give us wisdom, Lord, and let vengeance be Yours."

Brey joined in, as I went into hysterics. Stetson applied first aid as we waited for Jeff, and by the time the doctor arrived, I was in Stetson's arms.

"We'll get everything cleaned up," Lacey assured me as Jeff wheeled me onto the sidewalk after establishing that I didn't need to go to a hospital. She walked beside the wheeled bed for a few steps before falling back, promising to call Aubrey.

THE NEXT THING I knew Jeff was almost done giving me stitches.

"Nine total," he told me, quietly setting his surgical scissors down on the tray next to him. His eyes, the color of light brown sugar, were kind as he assessed me, checking my reflexes and studying the X-ray he'd taken of my back.

"Nothing broken, and I'm certain nothing is torn either," he said softly. "But you'll have a nice bruise back there for a couple of weeks. I pulled some slivers of glass out of it, but they only left superficial cuts, so they'll be healed up in a few days." Showing me the three small blue shards he'd removed that matched none of the broken dishes in my home, he suppressed a yawn before reaching for his clipboard.

As he took notes, I looked around the small room we were in, its pale blue walls a soothing color to my aching eyes. Charts of the human body covered the back of the door, and the faucet in the corner had a slow drip that made me wince. The smell of antiseptic made me want to vomit, but once Jeff finished administering pain killers, I found myself going in and out of consciousness. Soon nothing bothered me, except for constantly being woken up.

By the time morning arrived, I was feeling better and was able to hold down the yogurt Brey brought over. Terri, she told me, was on her way back from Houston and would probably make the three-hour drive in less than two. Stetson had called her after securing the crime scene.

"What about Aubrey?" I croaked out, the taste of strawberry lingering in my mouth. "Did Lacey get through to her?"

Brey nodded, earrings swaying. Her braided hair pulled at her temples, highlighting the black circles under her eyes. "She did. They had just landed in New York when Lacey called. They were ready to get on the next flight back, but Lacey told them we have everything under control."

The attempt I made to raise an eyebrow failed. "Do we?"

Brey nodded as Jeff entered the room, his sneakers quiet on the tile flooring. "Stetson called for reinforcements, so in about an hour, this town will be swarming with cops."

Standing, she nudged the wheeled stool toward Jeff. "I've gotta open the bakery, but I'll be back once we close if you're still here."

"I have to cancel my appointments," I said, trying to sit up. "I've got sessions all day! What time is it?"

Brey rushed over to me, pushing me down. "Cool it," she said, hands gentle but firm as she placed them against my shoulders. "Jeni took care of everything already. We found your planner among the mess in your office and called all the clients who were booked for today, tomorrow, and Wednesday."

Settling back into bed, I gave a sharp exhale as Jeff smoothed my hair away from my head wound, muttering under his breath as he poked at it.

"Listen to Jeff, Misty," Brey said, her tone imploring as she edged for the door. "Don't do anything stupid like trying to get out of bed until he tells you, okay?"

The wave I sent her was weak, and I found myself dozing off again as Jeff finished redressing my injury. Stetson arrived an hour later for his interview, waking me, and just as he was leaving, a vase of roses now sitting on the table next to my bed, Terri rushed in. Tan pants wrinkled, her shirt sported a large brown coffee stain on the right breast pocket. She looked exhausted.

"Misty," she cried, pulling me into her bosom after nearly knocking Stetson over with her large purse. "Between you and Aubrey, I've grown more gray hair in the last six months than I have in four years."

Finally pulling away, she patted my cheeks. Tears filled her hazel eyes even though I repeatedly assured her I'd be fine. Stetson had slipped out of the room to do a briefing with the several officers who'd just arrived at the station, mumbling something about needing a cup of coffee.

Voice trembling just a bit from my pain meds, I told her about Royce accidentally setting the books on fire. She shook her head, her no nonsense sneakers giving a slight squeak as she paced the small room.

"For such a small town, we're seeing a pretty big spike in crime," she mused. "And if you want my opinion, I think we aren't even scraping the surface of how deep this goes."

She gave me a worried look before leaving, and I wondered if she was right. Flamingo Springs is a small town, but the crimes we were experiencing reeked of a big city. Apparently, Stetson thought so, too, as he'd called in as much backup as he could. The hotel, Jeff told me later that afternoon as he'd filled out my release form, was filled to the max with federal agents, as it was suspected a well-known drug ring was behind the crime.

The rest of the day was a blur of signing forms, collecting what clothing I could from my trashed apartment, and moving into Lacey's spare bedroom. The only memory I had of the FBI agent who interviewed me was the light scent of lilac in my room, and I found myself struggling to remember my own birthday.

Stetson was in and out most of the day, visiting me twice at the clinic and twice at Lacey's, making sure I was settled in. His features settled into a grim look, his dark eyes narrow. And once I was positive I saw a glint or two of tears.

By seven that night I was curled in the twin-sized bed in Lacey's apartment, the smell of her cold cream drifting through the doorway as she moved around in the living room, her soft voice a comforting hum as she talked into her phone.

Icepack on my wound, I closed my eyes, Mitch's low tone soothing my headache. It'd taken quite a bit of protesting to convince him to stay in L.A. and not fly out to see me. I could hear Kasey talking in the background.

"Are you sure you're okay?" Obviously worried, Mitch fussed about flying out anyway to come take care of me.

I let out a soft laugh, wincing as I did so. "I'm fine, Mitch. Jeff said give it three or four days, and I'll be good as new. And besides, Lacey is taking care of me. There's no better place I could be than with her right now."

"If you're sure ..." Still sounding doubtful, Mitch paused before continuing, "I just wish we were there, like when everything happened with Mabel."

"Well, unless you can jar my memory, there's nothing you can do right now," I told him. "Hopefully everything will come back in the next few days, but until then, what happened is just a blur."

"How's your back?" Kasey asked.

Mitch had turned the phone on speaker, and I imagined the tall YouTuber pecking away at his laptop, taking notes while inhaling some sort of food.

"Quite sore, thanks for asking," I sighed. "One of the attackers kicked me right in the small of it, and there's a decent bruise there. Jeff had to pull shards of glass out it, so there's a few cuts too."

"Tell me about that," Kasey pressed.

I concentrated, the click-clack of typing filling my ear. "See, that's the weird thing. The shards are a really pale blue, but none of my dishes were that color. Stetson is trying to figure out where they're from, but so far, no such luck."

"Hmm." Mitch cleared his throat. "Any idea what kind of glass?"

"Jeff said they look like porcelain, if that helps," I said, shifting so that I was laying on my side, pulling the cinnamon-scented covers up to my cheek. "But I don't know of anywhere that would come from."

"What about the coloring on them?" Mitch's voice faded as he moved away from the phone. "Do they look painted or like that's the actual color of the glass?"

"I'm not really sure," I admitted. "Jeff showed them to me, but my vision was pretty blurry this morning, so I couldn't tell."

"That's okay," Kasey said. "Not trying to interrogate you, just looking for as many clues as we can, which isn't many, since we're so far away."

"And I'm thankful for your help," I told the pair warmly, my words cut off by a yawn.

"We should let you rest," Mitch said, and Kasey agreed before Mitch continued, "but is it okay if I talk to you for minute before I let you go?"

Hearing the change in his tone, I carefully rolled over onto my back, suddenly awake. "Of course. Is everything all right?"

"Hold on." The sounds of walking filled my ear as Mitch left his room, and, after a moment, he spoke.

"Everything's fine, but I wanted to talk about us. Maybe this isn't the best time, and I understand if you don't want to right now."

"No," I assured him. "I've been wanting to talk about us too."

"Good." Mitch's voice was filled with relief. "I'm assuming about the same thing?"

"That I like you as a dear friend, but I'm not in love with you but am really struggling to figure out how to say it?" Tone filled with irony, I let out a small laugh.

"Those words, exactly," Mitch chuckled. "I'm glad we're both on the same page."

"I do wish you were here, though," I sighed. Cutting off his offer to catch the next flight, I went on, "This case is so much crazier than what happened with Mabel, Mitch. There are a lot more people involved, and it's not an internal thing anymore. This is so much bigger than last time, and with Blaze and Aubrey gone, I think Stetson is drowning a little bit."

"I agree," Mitch said. "Kasey and I will keep going over everything you've told us and see what we can find out. Right now, I think those pieces of glass are a pretty big clue, if we can just figure out where they're from."

"I know I've seen them before." Stifling another yawn, I groaned and scrubbed a hand down my face. "Just can't remember where."

"Pray about it," Mitch suggested. "And though I know this isn't helpful advice, stop stressing, if you can. No matter what the outcome of all of this is, God's in control, so when He's ready for you to remember, you will."

After discussing the case a bit more, Mitch said a quick prayer for me before bidding me goodnight.

Turning out the light after plugging my phone in, I snuggled under my blanket, thankful we were still friends even after deciding to no longer pursue a relationship. Not long after that, I fell asleep as the sounds of Lacey moving around in the kitchen faded away and peace surrounded me, the sound of Mitch praying still filling the room.

9

The next day found me dressed by eight, my mind much clearer, my headache only a faint throbbing in the back of my eyes. After carefully hiding my bandage with a colorful bandana, I let myself out. Lacey had been gone since seven, and I made sure to lock the door after myself with the key she'd given me.

I wandered over to Aubrey's diner, ravished for something unhealthy. Since Lacey's cupboards had only offered oatmeal and a packet of banana chips, I'd decided to treat myself.

It'd been a struggle to find something comfortable to wear. The waistband of my pants caused pain to shoot up my spine. Finally settling on a maxi dress I'd grabbed from my closet, I paired it with bright pink flipflops that were covered in sequins. Unless one looked closely, the edge of the bandage that poked out from beneath my bandana wasn't noticeable, and my concealer stick did a good job of hiding the dark circles under my eyes.

"Ma'am," a tall, handsome man said, holding the door to the diner open for me. His green eyes raked up and down my figure, and his lips parted in a grin, revealing a front tooth with a small chip in it. I blushed, remembering him from the last time he'd been in town.

Cade had been one of the agents the FBI sent down to interview everyone after Mabel's arrest. From what I remembered, he possessed a great sense of humor and wasted no time in hitting on Aubrey.

"Thank you," I told him as we took a seat at the counter. The scents of maple syrup, coffee, bacon, and a dozen other delicious things swirled around us.

Looking around the diner as I waited for Brey to take my order, my left eye squinted a bit in the light. The sound of satisfied customers made a happy hum that rose and fell along with the clink of silverware.

Abigail Richards was seated in a small booth to my left, a cup of coffee and a stack of pancakes on the table in front of her. Forking a bite of the sweet breakfast food into her mouth, she typed on the keyboard of the small laptop that sat next to the coffee cup.

She seemed oblivious to the world around her, including the admiring glances she received from the agent who was seated at the table next to her booth. As if sensing my gaze, she glanced up. A small smile touched her lips and then she looked back at her laptop, a frown creasing her forehead as she stabbed the backspace key.

"Feeling better?" Brey asked, standing in front of me, the counter between us as she pulled a notebook from her apron pocket and clicked open the pen she held. Blond hair pulled back into a tight bun, she had a smear of maple syrup down the left side of her apron and a grease stain on the sleeve of her shirt.

Glancing at Cade, she gave him a bored stare when he winked at her. "Coffee, right?" she asked him, not waiting for me to answer her first question. "And the Mountain Man Bowl?"

Chuckling, he held her gaze, obviously interested. "You remembered."

Brey snorted, rolling her eyes. "Right. You and every other agent who stepped foot in here this morning have ordered the same thing."

Pen scratching across her order pad, she turned back to me.

"I think I'd like the Everything Plate," I told her, and she stopped writing. "And a glass of tea, if you've got some brewed," I added.

"Misty," she began, "you do know that the Everything Plate is, well, it's everything!"

"Brey, I'm starving." I gestured toward where Seth sat across the diner, scraping his Everything Plate clean. "If he can do it, I think I can too."

Brey laughed, shoving the order pad in her pocket after tearing off the ticket. "I'm glad you're feeling better," she said before she whirled away, yelling, "Terri, fire up the other griddle and empty the fridge! We've got an Everything order!"

Next to me, Cade chuckled. His eyes followed the pretty waitress as she zoomed around the diner, refilling glasses and mugs, handing out plates of food, and clearing tables as well as manning the register while Terri cooked everything. Hearty laughter rang out as she took care of agent after agent. She reminded me of Aubrey, and I nudged Cade with my shoulder as he stirred a creamer into his coffee.

"Forget it," I told him. "She's not only in a relationship, but she's also way too young for you."

Eyes glinting, he started to speak, but my attention was drawn away to the door where a woman stood, looking around the diner for a place to sit. Thin black hair that held a faint curl hung around her drawn face, and she seemed frightened, as if she might bolt at any minute.

She seemed familiar, and after sending her a friendly wave, I patted the empty seat next to me.

After a moment's hesitation, she edged toward me, eyes darting about nervously. Her worn sneakers scuffed the floor as she let out a cough. Her jeans had seen better days, one knee sporting a tear, and her turtleneck was two sizes too big for her thin frame. Carrying a small, scuffed up purse, the scar on the back of her hand seemed fresh, its pink color stark against her pale skin.

Slowly sitting on the stool next to me, she clutched her purse to her chest as I introduced myself, turning my back on Cade.

The woman paused before facing me, and as I stared into her green eyes, it occurred to me who she was just as she spoke.

"I'm Cynthia."

The smile she offered me was small, but despite the red scabs that dotted her gaunt face and the fine lines of stress that fanned out from her mouth, her eyes were clear. This was the woman who claimed to be Ryan's girlfriend. Studying her, I could see the resemblance between her and the photo she used as her profile picture.

"I'm Misty." Extending my hand, I gave her a gentle smile.

Taking it, she gave it a slight shake, her own hand cold and clammy.

"Ryan told me about you," she said, coughing into her elbow. "He thought you were awesome, and to be honest, I'm a bit of a fan of your YouTube channel."

Blushing, I was about to answer when Brey plunked my platter of food down in front of me right after setting down Cade's mixing bowl sized meal.

"All right, y'all," she bellowed above my head, and the diner fell silent. "Listen up! You've ate the diner out of pretty much everything, so unless one of you fine agents is willing to drive to Tumble to pick up supplies, the only thing I'm able to serve from here on out is pancakes and syrup."

A loud groan filled the air as the agents protested. Brey shrugged. "I can't help it. We're not in tourist season right now. You guys have eaten me out of a week's worth of supplies, and Jesse's Market only has so much!"

"I'll go!" One of the agents jumped to his feet. "Give me a list, and I'll pick everything up. Don't leave me to feed myself. I'll starve!"

Laughter filled the room, and as Brey filled out a shopping list, I turned back to Cynthia, noticing her gaze was on my food. Shaking her head when I offered her some, she bit her lip to hold back a cough, scratching viciously at her arm.

"Are you okay?" Cade asked, leaning around me. He eyed my food before refocusing on Cynthia, and I couldn't blame him. When Aubrey created the Everything Plate, she'd literally put everything on it. Bacon, sausage, ham, potatoes cooked two different ways, eggs, pancakes, muffins, and miniature waffles covered my plate, as well as two biscuits and a small serving of strawberries.

Cynthia nodded, eyes watering, and she slid off her stool. "I thought I was hungry," she said, fiddling with the straps on her purse, "but on second thought, I think I'll just find something small at the grocery store."

Catching her arm as she moved past me, I dropped my fork to the counter, where it landed with a clatter. "Wait! Do you have a place to stay?"

Cynthia halted, staring at me, and for a moment, it was almost as if her eyes were pleading for help. "Yes, I booked a room at the hotel. But thanks for asking."

Pulling away from me, she almost ran out the front door, as if I'd frightened her with my concern.

Cade took a sip of coffee. "I don't know what was more evident," he mumbled into his cup. "Her guilty conscience or the meth use."

Twisting around, I stared at him. "You can't be serious."

Forking a bite of cheesy hash browns into his mouth, he shrugged. "I am. She's got all the classic signs of it. The scratching, the scabs on her face, not to mention the coughing." Taking another swig of coffee, he swallowed. "Her hair is thinning too. Obviously, it could be a health condition, but I've worked enough drug-related cases to know when someone's using. And trust me, she's using."

"Something tells me Ryan's murder is connected to it," I said softly, leaning toward Cade, my platter of food forgotten.

Cade tucked back into his meal, and I took a moment to study him. Dirty blond hair neatly styled, he smelled faintly of tobacco and something spicy. Eyes dipping lower, I noticed the small scar beneath his ear before glancing at the edge of a tattoo that peeked out above his collar.

"Bullet graze," he said, and my eyes flicked to his. "The scar by my ear. Happened about four years ago. I thought for sure my number was up."

"God's not done with you," I said. "That's usually what something like that means."

Cade twisted his lips, looking past me for a moment when a fork scraped loudly against a plate. "Maybe. Or maybe I was just lucky." Reaching out, he dragged my platter across the bar until it sat in front of him. "If you aren't gonna eat this, I will."

Shaking my head, I handed him my napkin. "I thought I was hungry, but ..."

Cade nodded as he dove into the stack of pancakes that were heavily drizzled with espresso syrup.

"I get it. Coming face to face with what drug addiction really looks like can turn your stomach. Like looking a demon right in the face."

Snagging the coffee pot Brey left on the counter, he refilled his cup. "Honestly, Misty, the best thing you can do is forget about this case. You've been hurt once. You keep nosing around, and you're liable to get killed."

Nudging his foot with mine, I handed him a packet of creamer. "You've been talking to Stetson, haven't you? I've done nothing wrong, and I'm not going to stop. If anything, getting attacked like that has made me even more determined to find out who's behind all this and bring them to justice."

Cade leaned forward as an agent reached past him for a saltshaker. "Didn't you break into the guy's apartment?" he asked, pinning me with a pointed look.

Snatching a piece of bacon off the platter that was getting emptier by the second, I took a bite. "No evidence," I said, winking.

Pouring more syrup onto his waffles, he laughed. "You're my kinda woman, Misty."

The sounds of someone coming to a stop behind my stool cut off the rest of his words. Before he even spoke, I knew Stetson was standing behind me. The scent of hay and mint surrounded me. Turning, I started to crack a witty joke, but stopped at the sight of him.

His hazel eyes were tired, wrinkled shirt spotting a coffee stain. The smile he gave me was thin, and his shoulders were slightly slumped.

"Can we talk?" he asked, voice hoarse. Nodding at the agent sitting next to me, he heaved a sigh. "Hey, Cade."

"You okay, Stetson?" Cade asked, concerned. "You sound rough. Look it too."

Stetson cleared his throat. "I'll be fine. Just need some

coffee." Looking back at me, he rested one hand on the butt of his gun, a habit I wondered if he was aware of. "I need to see you. Can you come to the office?"

"Sure. Just let me pay Brey—"

"I got it," Cade told me. When I protested, he clinked his fork against the now empty platter. "No, it's only right. I'm the one who ate it."

Thanking him, I slid off the stool and followed Stetson, who held the door open for me. Stepping out on the sidewalk, I winced in the sunlight, sharp pain stabbing my eyes. The first few steps I took were a bit unsteady, and Stetson rested his hand on the small of my back, leg brushing against my skirt as we walked toward the police station.

Black SUVs and sleek cars lined the street, and agents could be seen here and there, talking to people, taking notes, or, in one agent's case, helping Abigail wash the front windows of her store while Vincent and Marie pointed out smudges.

Glancing up at Stetson as we walked, I was more than a little aware of the warm hand pressing against my back, the heat of it soothing against my bruise. Jaw moving ever so slightly as he chewed a piece of gum, he glanced at me, and I had the sudden urge to reach out and smooth away the lines that fanned out from his eyes.

When we reached the station, he looked down at me, and something in my heart paused at the emotion in his eyes. Normally hazel, they darkened to the color of coffee, and when he turned toward me, resting his hands on my waist, I didn't stop him. People bustled past us on the street, going about their last-minute business before the holiday, but for how much attention I paid them, we could have been completely alone.

"I could have lost you," Stetson said quietly. I placed a hand on his forearm, his skin smooth against my palm. "Misty, I could have lost you." Touching his forehead to mine, his breathing grew ragged, and I pressed my free hand against his chest, feeling his heartbeat.

"But you didn't," I whispered, knowing that everything in my life was about to change. "Stetson, I'm okay."

The laugh he let out was strangled, and something wet trickled down my temple as Stetson fought to hold his emotions in check.

"Misty, you mean so much to me," he finally said, pulling back, hands tightening on my waist. "My dad has always told me that my hard head and pride are my greatest downfall. They come in handy when you're on the back of a bucking bull or when you're trying to chase down a criminal, but they don't work so well when you love someone."

Meeting his sober gaze, I fought back my own tears. "And yet, here we are. In each other's arms, crying in the middle of town."

"Perhaps not the best time for this," Stetson said dryly. "But I've never been good at this stuff."

"I couldn't tell," I joked, wrinkling my nose at him. "But I wouldn't have it any other way. To know that what I feel for you is returned, to know that I haven't been going crazy, I've just been falling in love ..."

Stetson nodded. "Exactly. I've spent so many nights wide awake lately, and I wanted this moment to be so much than this."

Lowering my hands to his arms, I let out a chuckle. "Nah, I think this fits us perfectly. In the middle of a case, FBI agents storming the town around us while everyone watches us from their windows ... this is exactly how it should be. Crazy."

"Speaking of crazy," Abigail called from down the street, cupping her hands around her mouth as the agent continued to scrub her windows under Marie's instructions, "don't you think it's about time to kiss or something? Or is that too wild for you two, and you'd prefer to keep talking?"

"Ah, give them a break," Vincent said as he stood next to her, picking at his teeth with a toothpick. "Neither one of them are good with their emotions."

"And Misty being a counselor," Marie said disapprovingly as she pointed out another smudge to the agent.

"Oh, the irony," Abigail droned, dropping her hands to her sides.

"You're not helping, you know," Stetson called back.

I pulled away from his embrace, cheeks warm.

"Ruined the moment, did we?" Vincent teased.

"I sure hope so," Abigail interjected, and I felt myself warming to the new business owner. "Kinda lame to declare your love in the middle of the street. At least do it when it's raining, like in the movies."

"That's it!" Almost tripping over Stetson's foot, I jerked the door to the police station open. "I can't take anymore."

Following me, Stetson's normally tan cheeks were pink. Shutting the door behind us, he turned, halting when he saw that Chase and Terri were both staring at us with grins.

"You owe me lunch, kid," Terri said to Chase from the corner of her mouth.

"I do not," Chase argued, grabbing a highlighter from the coffee cup on his desk. "That was if they kissed."

"A muffin, then," Terri bargained. "Because there was a declaration of love."

"Fine by me," Chase agreed. "But you owe me coffee, because I said it would be awkward, and boy was it ever."

Hands pressed to my cheeks, I fled the room to Stetson's office as laughter filled the air. The shrill sound of the phone on Terri's desk cut through it. Flopping into the leather chair across from his desk, I wanted nothing more than to disappear into the floor.

"So," Stetson said as he shut the door, boots scraping on the hard wood flooring, "that was uncomfortable." Moving past me, he sat behind his desk, pushing his computer mouse to one side to wake the monitor.

Looking up from studying my feet, I noticed the wanted posters that hung on the board behind him, the black of the page borders stark against the cream-colored walls.

"You think?" I asked him dryly. "I haven't been that embarrassed since the time my mom decided it would be cute to sign me up as a bowl of peas in the Thanksgiving play her country club put on."

Stetson gave me an odd look as he tapped a command out on his keyboard. "I'm not following. What's the big deal about that? We were all in plays at some point during our childhood."

I pinned him with a steady look. "I was seventeen, and it was a play made up of five-year-olds."

Stetson bit his lower lip, struggling to stifle a grin. "That's pretty embarrassing." Leaning forward, he rested his forearms on top of the large calendar that covered much of the top of his desk. "I have to say, I didn't know people have been taking bets about us."

Waving a hand in the air, I slouched back into my chair. "It doesn't surprise me. We took bets about Audrey and Blaze, so why should it be any different with us?"

Stetson shook his head, making an exasperated face. "Cuz we're boring? And I thought the inhabitants of Flamingo Springs were sane." He drummed the fingers of his right hand on the top of his left forearm. "Speaking of inhabitants, Cynthia may have been his girlfriend, but she can't be trusted in her current state of mind, so be careful around her, okay?"

"How do you know I talked to her?" I asked, surprised, crossing my legs.

Stetson's eyes followed my movements, and after a pause, he answered, "I knew the moment Cynthia got to town—Terri told me she'd be coming. She'd already briefed me on how she suspects Cynthia is a meth user."

Biting the inside of my cheek, I smoothed a hand down my skirt. "I just wish you could arrest Royce and get this over with."

Stetson laughed. "If only things were that simple. We don't even know if he's done anything wrong. We've got a lot of circumstantial evidence on him and nothing more. Right now, I'm going on what I have, which is that drug use and most likely the creation and distribution of it are the reason Ryan was murdered in the first place. Big gang activity is nothing to be played with, and that's exactly what we're dealing with."

"I don't see how I can help with anything." Leaning forward, I grabbed a peppermint candy from the chipped dish that sat on the edge of his desk. "I can't remember anything from the past few days. I don't even remember my own phone number!"

Clearing his throat, Stetson's eyes narrowed as he glanced at my head, noting the piece of bandage that was sticking out from underneath my bandana.

"Yeah, I can understand that. And your computer and phone were so destroyed we couldn't get anything off them, but Jeni must have had an idea what you were looking at. She sent me a text this morning. Said to ask you about a number sequence."

"What number sequence?"

Stetson eyed me, and I could see he was struggling to hide his concern. "Misty, how much do you remember of the last few days?"

Shrugging, I touched my bandaged head with gentle fingers. "Honestly, the last week is in bits and pieces. I remember teaching a handful of lessons, meeting the girls for lunch, and I remember planning how to get a look at Ryan's apartment, but other than the fight we had, everything else is just a blur of faces, noises, and smells."

"So, you don't remember anything from the night you broke into Ryan's?" Stetson clarified, and I nodded.

"Right. I know I was working on my computer the night I was ..." Paling, I took a deep breath, stretching my toes as I scrubbed my flipflop across the scuffed floor. "The night I was attacked. But nothing else."

Stetson cleared his throat again, one eye squinting as he grimaced.

"I didn't realize your head wound was that bad." Stabbing a key on his keyboard, he looked back at me, black hair stirring when the vent above us began blowing out cool air. "I'll give Jeni a call and see if she has those numbers." Writing something down on a sticky note, he clucked his tongue. "I already took your statement, but there are one or two things I wanted to go over with you about your assault."

A tremble went through me at the mention of my attack, and I took a deep breath.

"Firstly," Stetson said, hazel eyes dark, "you said you remember being kicked in the back. As you know, the bruise on your lower back looks like the end of a square toed boot, and there were shards of blue porcelain in the wound."

Mouth going dry, I twisted my fingers in my lap as I remembered how helpless I'd felt as I'd lain on my kitchen floor, hearing my home being destroyed. Distress obviously evident on my face, Stetson shoved his chair back and came around his battered desk, sitting in the chair next to me and resting a hand on my knee.

"Misty, do you need to talk to someone?" he asked softly. "We can set you up with a licensed therapist if you want."

Closing my eyes for a moment, I took a deep breath before looking back at the deputy. "I don't think so. I just don't like thinking about what happened."

Stetson nodded. "I can understand that. But don't hesitate to get help if you need it. If you want to talk, you can see me, or I can set you up with someone. You know better than anyone the importance of not ignoring your emotions."

Shifting, he went back to his original thought. "What I wanted to say is that if you see anyone with square toed boots, make note of who they are and get away from them. I know there are lots of guys who wear boots like that, but it's not a super common shape this side of Texas, so if you see them, there's a good chance they're a suspect."

Dragging my chair next to his, he covered my shaking hands with his warm ones. His bronze-colored skin stood out against my pale fingers, and I noted the long scar on the back of his hand, his thumbnail black at the base from obviously pinching it in something.

"The second thing I wanted to say is I want you to spend Thanksgiving with me."

Head jerking up, I immediately regretted the quick movement. "Whoa! We confessed our feelings less than twenty minutes ago! Don't you think you're moving a little fast?"

Eyes crinkling at the corners, Stetson grinned. "Keeping an eye on the clock, are we?" he teased. Raising his voice, he spoke over my protest as I started to blush again. "I'm kidding. No, the reason I want you to spend Thanksgiving with me is for protection." Holding up a hand, he halted my words. "Let me finish. Misty, you always spend your holidays alone. Not only is that a super lonely thing to do, it's also not safe right now."

"It's not like I'll be alone," I argued. "This town as more FBI agents than a peacock has feathers!"

Stetson cocked his head. "That was a bit of an odd analogy. But I just think it would be for the best if you were out on the ranch. Like I've already said, we're dealing with a drug gang, and they've already targeted you once." The look he gave me was stern. "Besides, it won't be just the two of us. My dad will be there."

"Well, when you put it like that." Smiling, I pushed a strand of hair behind my ear. "I would love to spend Thanksgiving with you."

Something shifted in his gaze, a light of approval coming to his eyes, and he moved away from me. "It's settled then. Get your stuffed packed. I'll pick you up around two tomorrow."

Stetson stood, pulling me to my feet. His phone chirped. Rolling his eyes, he leaned forward and pressed his lips to my forehead in a soft kiss before stepping back.

Reaching out to twist the doorknob, I was stopped by his sudden inhale,

"Get away from the door." Voice harsh, he stared his phone, thumb moving over the screen. Holding the phone to his ear, he pointed at the chair I'd just vacated. "Sit."

Stabbing his fingers through his hair, he nodded at something the person on the phone said. "Cade, this is Stetson. I know what the numbers were that Ryan wanted me to find." Pausing, he twisted his lips, listening to Cade say something.

"It's worse than that. They're inmate numbers from the prison."

Stetson met my gaze as I sank into the chair, one hand going over my mouth as an acidic feeling flooded my stomach. The smell of flowers from the bouquet Stetson had given me filled my nose as memories of the night of my attack flooded my mind, the delicate blossoms crushed underfoot by my attackers.

The sound of dishes shattering while a voice whispered threats in my ear filled my mind, and a shiver went through me.

"Right. I'll forward the text to you, but I think I already know who they are." Pausing again, he gritted his teeth, moving to stand behind his desk. "Yeah, I think it's those guys too. You said a K-9 officer was on the way, right? Good. Listen, I'm taking Misty with me to my ranch for the next few days. Right."

Nodding, Stetson leaned down and pressed a few keys on his computer. "Yes, call Stan and let him know what's going on. Yeah, I'll get ahold of Blaze."

Straightening, he met my eyes again. "No, I'll talk to Cynthia. You just make sure she doesn't leave town." He held the phone away from himself and tapped a button on it, ending the call with Cade.

"Those numbers you found at Ryan's are inmate numbers," he said, tone blunt. Staring at me, he waited for my reply, a vein pulsing in his temple.

Sharp pain wove itself through my left eye as little bits and pieces of my memory returned, and I blinked, forcing my tears back. Blurry memories of what Ryan's apartment looked like, and fragments of the Bible study Jeni gave me while I'd snooped floated around my head. I struggled to understand them.

"So, I'm guessing I'm going to your ranch a day early?" I pressed against the back of my chair as I finally connected the dots, though I was still unable to remember much of that night and the day that followed.

Stetson nodded. "Right."

"That's why Ryan was so insistent you get those books," I said when Stetson remained silent. "He knew he couldn't just write down the names of the men who were after him, and he couldn't call you, either, as his phone was probably tapped."

"My guess is they were watching him too," Stetson agreed,

not looking up from the note he was jotting across a piece of paper, having sat back down. "And that's why he couldn't come to the station, either."

"But why go through all the trouble with the books? Why create such an intricate mess instead of just getting help? That could have saved his life." I ran a hand across the back of my neck, the slight scent of my perfume teasing my nose. "And how would he have gotten them to you?"

Stetson looked up at me. A red light blinked on the phone that sat on his desk as Terri transferred a call to him. "Through you," he said softly.

"I don't get it."

"Ryan had a note in his pocket the day he was run over. It was a prompt to ask you to dinner." Stetson looked back down at his desk, pen scratching over paper as he made another note before he glanced at his monitor, typing something. "At first, I thought he liked you, but now that I know about the books and the numbers ..." He trailed off. "Under his reminder to ask you out was one to give you the books. I think Ryan was going to use you to warn me about what's been going on."

"Do you think he knew how much danger that would put me in?" I asked, fingers twisting into my skirt again.

"No. I don't believe he was thinking straight at that point. Ryan was scared, and you were his last option. You were the one person he knew he could trust to get the numbers to me. Makes very little sense, the way he went about everything. But, then again, he wasn't thinking clearly." Stetson rose to his feet and grabbed his hat off the filing cabinet behind him, placing it on his head. "Come on. I'll take you by Lacey's so you can pack."

Pushing myself up out of the chair, one hand went to my head as pain exploded into my left eye. "What are you going to tell everyone?" I asked. "If people are coming after me, they'll just follow me to your ranch."

Stetson grunted, moving past me to open the office door. "I know. That's why you're packing your stuff into a duffle bag and catching a ride to the airport with Terri. I just texted her to get you a flight to Idaho. There's a taxi waiting when the plane lands to take you to a yoga conference."

Looking up at him as I walked past him into the hallway. "But I'm not really going, right?"

Stetson nodded as we walked toward the reception room. "Correct. As we speak, one of the agents is setting up a fake website. The FBI usually has a couple thousand on hand that they can turn into whatever they need. To the unsuspecting eye, it'll look like a legitimate website, where you can even purchase tickets, browse testimonials, and click over to a Facebook and Instagram page."

"You think they'll go there trying to shut me up?" I asked quietly.

Stetson cleared his throat. "Yup. They were willing to let you go the first time, but now that we've really homed in on Royce, they'll want to cut their losses and start tying the loose ends up."

"I've got those tickets," Terri said as we entered the reception room.

Chase quietly spoke into his phone as he typed something.

Turning, she grabbed some sheets of paper from the printer behind her and handed them to Stetson. "She's all set to go."

Stetson took them from her, frowning. "Thanks. Anything new with Cynthia?"

Terri shook her head. "Our guy says she's been on the phone since she went into her room at the hotel. Said she was yelling at someone for a while, but she's not acting like she's leaving any time soon."

Stetson pursed his lips before giving a short nod. "Keep me up to date." Holding the door open, he looked at me. "Shall we?"

Stepping past him onto the boardwalk, I turned to face him as he followed me, shutting the door behind him. "I have a bad feeling about this," I told him. "I don't think this is going to work."

"What?" he asked, striding down the boardwalk.

I hurried to catch up to him. "This whole going out to your ranch thing," I answered, scratching my cheek when a tendril of hair drifted across it in the light breeze. "We did this last time, remember? With Aubrey? But she still ended up almost getting killed."

Stetson stopped, turning to face me, his face grim. "But unlike last time, it's only you coming out to the ranch. And unless my dad is the one making the hits on you, it'll be fine. I'll be there the whole time."

Biting the inside of his cheek, he looked down the street to where Abigail was now directing the agent in hanging up a small sign from the overhang of her store. Seth stood next to her, watching us.

"But you're right. I've got a bad feeling about it too."

We started walking again, and he cupped his hand around my elbow, guiding me. "Do you think Royce is really guilty, or are we way off track?" I asked, breathing in the slight scent of mint and lime, my headache starting to abate.

"Honestly," Stetson sighed, "I don't know. All the evidence is pointing to him. I found out this morning that he used to own a car that matches your description of the one that hit Ryan, but records show he sold it a while back to a friend. And we did a sweep of the store and the apartment and found nothing. If he's running drugs, he's hiding it pretty well, because we searched his car too."

"If we were in a bigger city, I'd say Ryan was just an innocent victim of a careless driver," I mused, waiting for Stetson to open the door to Lacey's store.

"So would I, but we're not."

We waved at Lacey as she scurried around her salon, talking a mile a minute to the young girl who sat in a leather chair, her dark locks almost hidden by aluminum foil. The quick wave she sent back was followed by a distracted smile as she checked her phone, and we made our way past her into the back room.

Stetson stayed in the living room while I quickly packed a duffel bag I found in Lacey's closet. I was careful to only borrow items that she didn't wear often.

"Flamingo Springs has been the quietest town in the state for years, and now in the span of just a few months, we've had two homicides, several attempted murders, and multiple crimes." Stetson leaned against the doorframe, watching me struggle to zip the duffle bag closed.

Glancing up at him, I nodded, worrying my lower lip. "Kinda scary, isn't it? How crime seems to settle in everywhere."

Stetson crossed his arms over his chest. "Sign of the times, I'd say." The rest of his words were cut off by the sound of a truck rumbling to a stop behind Lacey's salon. We shared a look, both recognizing the loud roar to belong to Cody Jackson's ranch vehicle.

"He picks the worst times," I commented, finally getting the duffel closed. Setting it on the floor, I smoothed wrinkles out of the quilt on the bed.

"Always." Stetson grinned at me. "I know they broke up for good over the summer, but seems like he can't accept she doesn't want him anymore." Grin widening, he gestured toward the living room. "Shall we eavesdrop?"

Chuckling, I followed him out of the bedroom and across Lacey's small living room the window she'd left partially cracked. "We shouldn't, really, but, why not?"

Standing on either side of the window, we peered into the opening behind Lacey's store and watched Cody climb down out of his black truck. Closing the door, he took a moment to straighten his shirt and smooth his hair before striding to the back door of the salon and out of our sight.

Sharing another look, Stetson and I held our breath as we listened, hearing Cody's low voice as he said something to Lacey. A moment later, the rodeo star reappeared, closely followed by Lacey.

"I'd say you have some nerve coming here, but you'd probably take that as a compliment." Lacey's voice was surprisingly controlled as she leaned against Cody's truck, hands at her side, black apron fluttering in the slight breeze that sprang up.

"I thought you'd be happy to see me." Standing a few feet away from her, Cody tucked his fingertips into his back pockets and rocked back on the heels of his boots, blond hair catching in the light.

"Why would I be happy to see someone I broke up with months ago?"

Lacey crossed her arms over her chest, and beside me, Stetson bit back a chuckle. Hitting his foot with mine, I gave him a warning glance. If we could hear them, they could hear us, and I would hate it if Lacey caught me invading her privacy.

"You don't mean that." Cody's short laugh was confident. "You aren't over me anymore than I'm over you."

"I assure you, I was over you the moment I walked away from you in July. That's what happens when you refuse to commit after someone gives you chance after chance—they get over you in a hurry and don't look back."

"Lacey Baker, lying doesn't suit you very well," Cody replied, unbothered by the stylist's rebuttal. "Your left ear always gets red when you lie, and right now it looks like it's about to catch on fire." Hands going to his sides, he took a step toward his on and off again love interest. "I want you back."

"Why? Your latest fling see you for who you really are?"

Lacey didn't move from her spot against the truck, and nudging Stetson with my shoulder, I pointed at her left ear. Even from a distance we could see how red it was. Though her words were strong, the slight quiver that filled them didn't escape me, nor did it get past Cody, for he let out a low laugh.

"She saw I was still in love with someone else."

"Yourself?" Lacey guessed, and this time it was my turn to muffle a giggle.

Stepping even closer, Cody stared down at her, shoulders tense. "I love you, Lacey. And I'm tired of running from it."

Finally moving, Lacey reached out and pressed her hand to Cody's chest. "So that's why you're coming to me now? Because you're tired? Not because of the usual reasons one confesses their love?"

Bumping my arm, Stetson leaned down, breath warm on my neck as he whispered, "She's been hanging out with you, hasn't she? She's got some great responses."

Smirking, I only shrugged before refocusing on the drama unfolding before us.

"Maybe because I'm scared of what I feel," Cody finally said after a long pause. "Maybe because I can't stop thinking about you. Can't stop hearing your laugh, hearing your cheer when I'm on the back of a bull, can't stop remembering how you feel in my arms, your lips against mine."

Lacey's once straight arm began to bend just a bit, and I let out a quiet groan. "No, don't weaken now. He's totally playing you."

"I don't think he is," Stetson whispered, shifting his weight. The floor squeaked slightly.

"Tell me you don't feel the same, and I'll leave you alone from here out." Leaning forward, Cody pressed against Lacey's hand, closing the space between them, palms braced against the truck on either side of her, trapping her.

"Cody, I don't feel for you anymore—I'm getting engaged." Lacey's voice was weak, hand still touching the cowboy.

"I said mean it," Cody whispered before dipping his head, kissing her.

Eyes meeting in a disgusted look, Stetson and I backed away from the window, giving the couple a moment.

"I can't believe she fell for that. Total emotional and attraction-based manipulation." Voice low, I threw my hands in the air, staring at Stetson.

Eyes gleaming as he opened his mouth to argue, Stetson was cut off when the sound of a slap filled the air.

Rushing back to the window, we peered down in time to see Cody falling back from Lacey, hand going to his cheek.

Hands on her hips, Lacey glared at him, the sequins on her shirt winking up at us.

"You're right. I don't mean it. And I never will. I'll never not love you with everything that I am, but you're toxic to me. You're poison to yourself, and I cannot, I will not, live my life constantly being hurt because you refuse to confront your past. So yes, I love you, but I love you too much to watch you destroy yourself time and time again and take me down with you."

Without waiting to hear his response, Lacey spun on her heel and stomped back to the salon. Mindful of the client who was still inside, she shut the door quietly, and Cody was left staring at her, hand still pressed against his cheek.

For a long moment, he stared after Lacey, shoulders drooping, before he climbed back in his truck and left. It wasn't until the rumble of his engine completely faded away that Stetson and I backed away from the window for the last time.

"So," I sighed. "That was heartbreaking to watch."

"Agreed," Stetson replied. "Makes me want to sit them both down and have them hash it out till it works, but I know that's not possible."

The chirping of his phone cut off his next words. Answering it, he headed back to my bedroom where he grabbed the duffel bag off the floor.

"This is Stetson," he said. After a moment, he chuckled. "Cade, you call me so much I'm starting to think you want a job." Motioning me to go back to the living room, he laughed again before sobering. "Yeah, we're all set to head out. You got everything set up? Good. Thanks."

Lowering the phone, he tapped a button before clipping it back onto his belt. "You ready? Coast is clear for you to head out to the ranch, and Terri will be here any moment to pick you up."

All thoughts of Cody and Lacey leaving my mind, I picked up my purse, my headache beginning to worsen.

"Something tells me this ordeal is far from over," I muttered. Glancing at Stetson as I moved toward the door, I saw that his jaw was tight.

"And something tells me we're about to find out that some of the people we think are our friends are really our enemies," he replied.

10

Stetson's dark words stayed with me, and I turned them over in my head on the ride to Stetson's ranch. Just like the case when Mabel had been running around trying to kill people, I knew something was off. We were missing something, and it could be a matter of life or death.

Sensing I was in no mood to talk, Terri remained quiet on the drive, occasionally flipping through radio stations until she found one she liked, a country station that blasted the oldies. Glancing at her from the corner of my eye as she focused on the road, I noted the way she pursed her lips when she looked in the side mirror before passing someone.

Terri is a wonderful person to be around and is much like a mother, friend, and cheerleader, all wrapped up in one sturdy package. If it hadn't been for her, I doubted I would have stayed in Flamingo Springs.

She had a way of showing up just when you needed some encouragement and could quote scripture better than most pastors. Though I knew very little about her past, except that she'd gone through a bitter divorce and joined the police force after a successful career as a loan officer, I considered her a close friend.

Her khaki pants and black shirt were neatly pressed and carried the slight scent of roses, and her wiry, gray-streaked brown hair was twisted back into a tight knot. If anything happened, she'd fight for all she was worth, and I knew that as long as I was with her, I was safe.

She slowed the vehicle to make a sharp right turn onto a dirt road that signified we'd entered Stetson's property and looked over at me as dust settled onto the windshield.

"I'll spare you the worn-out platitudes and greeting card scripture verses," she said. "Life will never be easy, and though I know this isn't something you asked for, all this crazy stuff that's been happening, you have to admit, it feels right."

Looking back at the road for a moment, she swerved to avoid a large rock, almost taking out a small cactus.

I took the time to wet my lips. "You're right," I told her. "Never would I have thought something like this would happen to me, but if I truly think about everything that's going on, it feels like I was meant for this. Whatever *this* is."

Shaking my head, I reached up a hand to scratch at the slightly itchy scab that had formed over my wound. "But I sure am ready for it to be over."

Terri brought the car to a stop in front of the tall gate that bore Stetson's last name and served as the only entrance to his property, the rest of his ranch surrounded by fencing. She nodded as she unbuckled her seat belt. "I bet you are."

Sliding out of her seat, she went around the front of the car to unlock the wrought iron gates with the keys Stetson had given her. After opening them, she drove the car through, then got back out and closed them. The click of the padlock was audible above the noise of the engine.

I folded my hands in my lap and looked out my window as she slowly drove down the dirt road. Having never been out to Stetson's ranch before, I wasn't sure what to expect. Though he hoped to one day retire from the force and make his living as a rancher, right now he only owned about twenty head of cows and spent his free time training horses. As we drew nearer to the house, Terri tapped the brakes to avoid hitting a chicken that darted across the road. A sense of peace settled into my stomach.

The man who'd been sitting in one of the rocking chairs on the white wraparound porch stood, waving to us as Terri brought the car to a stop.

"Y'all hungry?" he called out in a thick drawl as we got out. Dark hair streaked with gray, his hazel eyes crinkled at the corners just like his son's did when he grinned.

I smiled back. "Always," I answered as Terri stepped forward.

"Frank," she said, giving Stetson's dad a hug. "Haven't seen you in a while. You still running that charting boat?"

Frank nodded as he followed us to the back of the car to help with our bags, stepping over a curious chicken that was pecking at my foot. "Yep. Business is booming so much I decided to take a month or so off and come stay with Stetson. Boy's so busy he never takes the time to make a good meal, so I've been working on adding some meat to his bones."

Terri sniffed the air with a smile. "And from the smell of it, you've been cooking up a storm today."

Frank squinted in the bright sunlight as he shut the trunk and turned to me. "Got some good old Cajun gumbo on the stove and lobster biscuits in the oven."

Looking me up and down, he gave a nod of approval. "And you have to be Misty." He gave me a one-armed hug. "Stetson's said a lot about you."

"Hopefully good things," I replied, falling in step with him as he started toward the house, Terri on his other side.

"Of course," he chuckled. "Said you've got a weak spot for a good slice of pie, so I made a persimmon one. Hope you like it."

"She will," Terri assured him as we went up the steps onto the porch. An overhead fan sent a cool breeze down on us as Frank opened the screen door. "She might not look like it, but this girl will eat y'all out of house and home before the week is up."

Following Terri through the door into the foyer, I kicked off my sneakers before moving into the kitchen. Like most ranch homes, Stetson's floorplan was open, with high ceilings, wood flooring, and large windows. The kitchen was a cook's dream, with a marble island in the middle that Aubrey would love to use when she made candy at Christmas. The scent of gumbo and pie filled the air, and my stomach let out a loud grumble.

"Stairs are gettin' hard my knees, so I'm in the guestroom downstairs," Frank said as he moved past me and into the living room. "I took the liberty of cleaning up the spare room upstairs. Has plenty of room for your yoga and a desk if you need to work."

"Oh, that wasn't necessary," I protested, following him as he wheeled my luggage across the multi-colored rug that covered the floor between the leather couches and stone fireplace. "I'm happy to crash on the sofa."

"Nonsense," Frank huffed, reaching the stairs and shortening the handle on my suitcase. "My boy's got this massive home and only uses three rooms in it. Doesn't even have a dog to run around and stir the dust." Starting up the steps, he pulled the suitcase after him. "You have full run of this place while you're here. Maybe tonight after dinner we can dig through his stuff and find some Christmas decorations."

"I wouldn't want to pry," I objected. Steps squeaking under

my weight, I followed him. Terri stayed behind on one of the couches.

"No, no," came the reply. "Stetson's been existing in this place long enough. It's time he starts living, and that begins with decorating for Christmas." Frank's voice became muffled as he reached the top of the stairs and disappeared into the first room on the right. "Whether he wants to or not."

Hearing a thump as he set my luggage down on the floor, I joined him in time to see him take a deep breath, wiping a shaking hand over his suddenly sweaty forehead.

"Frank?" Setting my bags on the queen-sized bed, I gave him a concerned look. "Are you feeling okay? Do you need to sit down?"

Dropping his hand, Frank sent me a quick smile, dark eyes crinkled at the corners. "Ah, you know us age-challenged people, Misty. Can't keep up like the old days." He jutted his chin toward a door by the back of the room. "Bathroom's through there if you need to set anything up."

Leaving the room, he headed back to the stairs, and I stared after him. Frank wasn't that old, and the sudden change in his skin color and strength concerned me.

The sudden crunch of tires on gravel outside distracted me from further worrying for Stetson's father. I turned to the partially open window. A familiar truck eased to a stop amid a flurry of chickens, and after a moment, the driver's door opened and Seth stepped out.

For a moment, he simply stood and gazed around him. Then, as if sensing my eyes on him, he lifted his head and stared directly at my window. Remembering Stetson's warning that no one could know where I was, I stepped back, but Seth only turned to his vehicle, shutting the door as Frank crossed the drive to greet him.

"Stetson's down at the office, if that's who you're looking

for." Terri's voice drifted up to me as she joined Frank, one hand resting on her hip, only inches from the gun she carried on her belt at the small of her back.

Seth's reply was too low for me to understand, and Frank stepped forward, extending his hand.

"I don't think we've met," he said, and in his tone, I heard the same nonchalance that filled Stetson's when he was suspicious of something.

Seth introduced himself, shaking Frank's hand, but his attention seemed to be on Terri.

"Frank's an old friend of mine," she said, patting Frank on the arm. "Had to drop by and see him before he leaves."

The trio spent another minute exchanging pleasantries before Seth turned toward his truck, saying he'd catch Stetson at the station. The chickens that seemed to have lost interest the moment they realized he didn't have feed came scurrying back over, perhaps hopeful he'd have some now. Ignoring them, he instead looked back at my window, and once again, I stepped away, though I was sure he wasn't able to see me against the reflection of the bright sky.

My phone buzzed in my pocket. I turned away and headed into the bathroom.

A text from Mitch.

Any news on the case?

Letting out a sigh, I sent back a quick response.

Nope. But I'm under protective custody. Spending holidays at Stetson's ranch.

Mitch sent a concerned emoji with another text.

That didn't work out too well last time. You sure about this?

Not really. But Stetson said I'll be fine.

Keep me updated. And please be careful.

I told him that I would, but even as I hit send, a knot settled into my stomach. Somehow, I didn't think being careful would help me one way or another anymore.

"Dad, I think this has to be the best pot of gumbo you've ever made." Stetson leaned back in his chair directly across from me, letting out a contented sigh as he traced a circle on the table with his glass of sweet tea. Dark strands of hair fell over his forehead, and he grinned, the dimple in his cheek deepening as Frank laughed.

"You say that every year, and I always leave you the recipe." Frank spooned another bite of thick gumbo into his mouth. "I think the crayfish are what really brings it together."

"I'll second that," Terri said from beside me. Though she'd initially refused to stay for dinner, all it'd taken was one gentle glance from Frank for her to change her mind, and I wondered if there was more between the two than just friendship. Glancing at Stetson to see if he'd noticed the sparks between his father and his dispatcher, I found him studying me, hazel eyes squinted.

Suddenly warm, I spoke. "All I can say is I've eaten more tonight than in the last week, and I've still room for that pie. According to Terri, when Seth heard Frank had made one, I thought he was about to beg for a slice."

"Did Seth say what he wanted when he came out here?"

Stetson drummed his fingers on the table, the overhead light casting a yellow pallor onto the glass he'd finally pushed away.

Terri scraped her blue bowl with a spoon. "Said he had some questions about horse training and thought you were home already."

"He's never shown an interest in horses before and has no place for them, so it seemed a bit off," Stetson told her.

"Just being nosey?" I asked, sipping my tea. The cozy scents of food, Stetson's cologne, and gun oil surrounded me in a warm hug.

"Kinda the direction I'm leaning," Stetson answered. "He's getting on in years, and sometimes I worry his mind is slipping. He asked me the same question four different times and seemed a bit lost."

"Such a sweet man too," I murmured. "He helped me paint my studio."

"Age doesn't discriminate, sadly enough," Frank said, setting his spoon down. "But he did seem like a nice fellow. I think he might have a bit of a crush on Terri, though."

Rolling her eyes, Terri patted her mouth with a paper napkin.

"I assure you, nothing could be further from the truth," she laughed. "Seth is a sweet old man who's never met a stranger."

"I don't know about that," Stetson teased her, picking up his bowl and rising to his feet. "Dad might be on to something."

Standing, I mimicked his actions, waving at Terri and Frank as they followed suit, bickering over whether or not Seth liked the dispatcher.

"No, Stetson and I can clean up. You two go argue in the living room."

"Kinda obvious, aren't you?" Stetson mumbled as we carried everything into the kitchen and loaded the dishwasher.

"First, you seated them across from each other, now you're giving them alone time?"

Lips parting in a sly smile, I placed the dirty bowls on the bottom rack of the dishwasher.

We worked together in a comfortable silence. Frank and Terri's voices became distant as they left the room. Focused on wiping down the counters while Stetson set out saucers and cups for dessert and coffee, I almost jumped out of my socks when he pressed a hand to the small of my back to get around me to the silverware drawer.

My reaction wasn't lost to him, and he paused, turning to face me, a slow grin revealing white teeth. Attention drawn to the tiny scar by his lower lip, my heart thudded in my chest as he stepped closer, one hand holding four forks and a pie server, the other at his side.

"Never seems like the right time, does it?" he said, boots scuffing on the floor as he shifted. "Always something that comes up and kinda ruins the whole moment."

"I'm going to pretend you didn't just try to broach this subject with your dad sitting in the next room." Voice trembling a bit, I poured the coffee, eyes fixed on the tattoo on the underside of my wrist, watching the vein beneath it pulse.

"That would be awkward, wouldn't it?" Stetson let out a soft laugh as he sliced the pie. "But you know we can't run from this forever. Two years is a long time already."

Turning to face him, I placed a hand, made warm from the coffee pot, on his forearm and met his steady gaze. "We've made it these two years just fine, so I'm pretty sure we can hold on for a bit longer."

Before Stetson could respond, I picked up two of the coffee cups and disappeared into the living room just in time to catch Frank planting a kiss on Terri's cheek.

Busying myself with finding coasters to give the flustered

couple a moment to collect themselves, I wondered if now actually was a good time for Stetson and me to put our feelings on the table. Frank certainly wasn't having a problem doing so.

Ignoring Terri's bright red cheeks as she quickly moved to a chair opposite the couch and Frank's sudden interest in a ranching magazine, I headed back into the kitchen. Stetson finished placing slices of pie on the saucers, and I helped him balance the fourth one on his arm before grabbing the remaining cups of coffee. Returning to the living room, Stetson sat by Frank after passing out the pie and taking his cup of coffee from me.

I chose a spot on the ottoman next to Terri and took a sip, enjoying the bitter taste of chicory softened by a touch of creamer. Talk quickly turned to the case, and Frank mentioned his concern over the danger I was currently in.

"Have you had any leads at all with those prisoner numbers?" he asked his son.

Stetson nodded, speaking around a bit of pie. "With the help of the FBI, we've managed to track three of them into Galveston. The team leader is confident he'll have them in custody within the next forty-eight hours. We know this is a drug operation, most likely cocaine and meth, and that someone here in Flamingo Springs is heading the operation, or, at the very least, acting as a mule."

"Ryan?" Terri asked quietly, khakis rasping as she shifted in her chair.

"Possibly," Stetson told her. "But unlikely. I think he was part of it, but either unknowingly, or unwillingly. No, my thoughts are it's his brother, Royce, but his background check was clear, and we've searched the shop with a K-9 twice. Cade said they're going to sweep it one more time before calling it quits."

"So, at this point," I said, finishing my pie, "you're certain you know who it is, but you're just waiting for facts to line up."

"Exactly," Stetson replied.

Frank gave me a troubled look. The cackle of chickens suddenly grew loud as the flock moved past the window. "A dangerous game to play, if you ask me," he said. "First, that young shop owner got ran over and ended up passing from his injuries, then Misty was attacked and almost killed ..." Mouth set in a thin line, he gave his son a dark look. "I don't like it, Stetson. What makes you think she's safe out here?"

"In part is the fact that we've set a trap out of state that should lure a few of the criminals away," Stetson answered, meeting his dad's stare. "And also because she's out here with us."

"I do see your point," Frank interrupted, "but isn't this pretty close to what happened this past summer with Blaze and Aubrey?"

"Well," I interjected, "unless it's one of you three who are out to kill me, we won't have the same problem. No one would have ever suspected Mabel of being the killer."

This time it was me who Frank pinned with a hard look. "Don't try and deny you aren't having the same bad feelin', Misty."

"Dad," Stetson warned. "She's safe here. And it's almost Thanksgiving. Let's focus on that, okay?"

Frank agreed, but his words stayed with me because he was right. The feeling that he spoke of had been sitting in my stomach for the last twelve hours, and I feared this holiday season would be one not soon forgotten—and not for good reasons, either.

11

The day before Thanksgiving found Frank and me prepping the turkey that had been thawing in Stetson's fridge for four days, baking three kinds of pies, and arguing over the color of napkins to use.

Frank had brought almost everything he could think of from his kitchen back in Louisiana, including two different sets of cloth napkins. While I argued that cranberry was the better color to use, he leaned toward the brown, and we ended up laughing until we cried while we seasoned the turkey.

"You've really been a light during this time," I told Frank. "Stetson has no idea how blessed he is to have such an amazing father."

Frank gave me a long look as he rubbed salt into the pale skin of the turkey, his apron smeared with various spices and pie fillings.

"I wasn't always like this," he admitted. "Wasn't always so easy going. After his mother died, I was lost, and I stayed lost for a long time. I hated God, hated myself, and though I did my best, I wasn't a good father. That's why Stetson got into bull riding in the first place."

"Had to prove himself, I'm guessing," I said, leaning against the counter as Frank injected homemade mayonnaise under the turkey's skin with a cooking needle.

Frank gave me a startled look before chuckling. "I forgot you're a counselor. But yeah, he thought he had to be a star to matter to me. But he didn't have to do none of that to mean the world to me. It wasn't until he was twenty-two and busted his head open and almost died before I figured it out. That's when I got things right with the Lord."

"And now look at you." Crossing the kitchen, I opened the fridge so he could place the turkey back in. "You're one of the gentlest, kindest people I've ever met." I shut the fridge as he went to wash his hands, the smell of spices and pie filling my nose.

Frank sighed, lathering his hands. "I feel the same about you, Misty. I see you with my boy and ..." Voice trailing off, he looked down at his hands, rinsing them. "When I see you with Stetson, I see a beautiful future for you two. It's a future I've prayed over his life for six years."

Handing him a towel to dry his hands, I studied Stetson's dad. "I'm just not sure now is the right time."

The sound of the front door opening and closing as Stetson came in from feeding the cattle reached our ears, and Frank pinned me with a serious look, salt and pepper colored hair tousled.

"There never will be a right time, Misty. Not in the sense you're thinking. Don't waste your life waiting for the right moment, or the perfect setting, or the correct day. Do that, and you'll turn around and realize you've missed out on almost two decades of what could have been joy and fulfillment."

"Something smells great in here." Stetson's voice filled the room as he entered the kitchen. Socked feet silent on the tile floor, he padded past me and opened the fridge, peering inside.

"Look at all these pies," he mused as he straightened, holding the container with leftover gumbo. "Might just have one of those for lunch instead."

"Do that, and you won't see another Thanksgiving," his dad threatened him.

"Please." Stetson rolled his eyes. Filling a bowl with the southern soup, he placed it in the microwave then turned to face me. "Had a promising day. FBI nailed those three guys in Galveston and are currently interrogating them. I highly doubt two of them will give us any info, but the third? Cade told me he'll crack before dinner. He's just a kid and he really doesn't want to go back to prison. They've offered him a plea deal."

"God is good," I breathed, knees suddenly going weak. "While there's always a lot to be thankful for, this year I have even more so to be grateful for."

"Good timing right there," Frank muttered, but when I turned to glare at him, he was busy cutting Stetson a slice of persimmon pie from the day before.

"What does Blaze think of all this?" I asked Stetson, sitting down next to him at the kitchen table after filling a glass with water for him. "And Aubrey?" I frowned. "I hate not being able to talk to her right now."

"Well," Stetson drawled while Frank clanged around the kitchen, "he wishes he was here to handle it, but I can tell he's kinda glad not to be here at the same time. Aubrey said she's spending overtime in prayer over the whole thing and can't wait to talk to you."

"Do you think Blaze is going to propose on this trip? Or wait?" I asked, watching the longhorn tattoo on Stetson's bicep ripple as he spooned gumbo into his mouth. Pulling one foot up onto the chair, I rested my chin on my legging-clad leg, Lacey's oversized knit sweater soft against my skin.

"Nah," Stetson answered after a moment. "I think by Christmas he will, though."

"Oh, is that when the time is right?" Frank piped up from the edge of the kitchen as he came into the dining room and took his place across from me.

Giving him a bemused look, Stetson pushed his empty bowl away before laying his arm over the back of my chair. "I guess?" he said, tone questioning.

"Don't mind your dad," I said, face flushing as my sweater threatened to choke me. "I think he's just feeling tired today."

Frank gave me a dirty look. "I'm fifty-three, darlin'," he drawled. "Not eighty-seven."

"You have been actin' a little off, though," Stetson pointed out. "Gettin' out of breath and looking pale. Something you need to tell me?"

Rolling his eyes, Frank took a large sip of his iced tea, making sure to slurp. "Give me a break. I could run circles around you two any day of the week and twice on a Sunday. I'm fine."

Knowing he wasn't, I opened my mouth to tell him so but quickly closed it when I saw the warning gleam in his eyes. When he was ready, Frank would tell us what was going on.

We spent the rest of the afternoon finishing the prep work for the next day and playing the two boardgames Stetson found in his hall closet. Laughter often filled the house as we joked around, enjoying each other's company, and it was during the middle of making hot chocolate that Stetson received a call from Cade.

"We got a confession and have enough evidence to arrest Royce," the FBI agent told Stetson, who placed his cell on speakerphone. "Our K-9 unit found traces of illegal substances in the shop, and we were able to go from there. Y'all can go ahead and relax and have a good Thanksgiving. By this time next week, everything will be wrapped up, and Misty will be free to return home any time after tomorrow."

Hands raised in a silent hallelujah, I met Stetson's warm eyes, watching the tight lines by his mouth relax. Thanking Cade, he hung up and bent down to where I was on the couch, wrapping me in a tight hug.

"Lord, You are faithful," Frank prayed next to me as I breathed in the scent of Stetson's aftershave, arms going around his middle. "Your word is tried and true, and I thank You that Your eye has been on the little sparrow named Misty."

Tears filled my eyes and dampened Stetson's shirt as I stood, leaning against him as Frank continued to pray. Face still pressed into his firm shoulder, I lifted up my own praise, Stetson joining in. Though something told me this trial wasn't over just yet, peace filled me, God gently reminding me that even if the whole world fell apart, His word would still remain.

"I've really missed talking to you," I told Aubrey on the phone the next day, sitting cross-legged in the reclining chair in my room.

Midmorning light filtered into the cheery room, dust particles dancing through the beams as a light breeze blew outside. The hearty scents of roasting turkey, vinegar green beans, and other holiday dishes teased my nose, the sounds of Frank and Stetson moving about downstairs a pleasant backdrop to my three-hour conversation with my best friend.

"Girl," Aubrey breathed heavily into my ear, "when I tell you Blaze had to about tie me down to keep me from catching the first flight back ..." Voice trailing off, she took a sip of something. "I've prayed so much for you this past week that my knees are calloused."

Laughing, I thanked her. "And God heard you, because it's over, and tomorrow night, I can go home. With Royce behind bars, I can finally get back to my normal routine."

"Do they know if they'll get the other criminals involved?" Aubrey asked, voice holding just a hint of worry.

"Cade feels they're long gone. I trust him. He helped handle your case and did a great job, so I'm confident he won't let me down."

"Cade," Aubrey said drily. "I remember him. The one with the chipped front tooth and the tattoo on his neck, right? Yeah, he kept cracking the lamest jokes when I was in the clinic the morning after Mabel attacked me. I kept laughing at them, so I think that's why he told them nonstop."

"I'm just ready to go to the diner and have some of your pancakes," I said. "I love Frank and his cooking, but between you and me, you're my favorite cook."

"Is that Misty?" Blaze's deep voice cut off Aubrey's reply, and after a brief moment of static, he came on the line.

"Hey, Blaze," I said cheerfully, stretching my jean-covered legs out in front of me before pushing my hair out of my eyes.

"Misty," he replied. "You doin' okay? Stetson treating you right?"

"Really, Blaze?" Aubrey protested, but Blaze only laughed.

"He is," I assured the sheriff. "And he's done such a good job in your absence, I think you might be in trouble if he decides to run against you in the election."

"He'd have my vote," Aubrey said, which led to a playful argument between her and Blaze.

"Listen, you two," I said between chuckles, "why don't I let you go continue this fight and go help Frank with the food?"

"Before you go," Blaze said, his tone turning serious, "there's actually something I need to tell you."

"Oh?" I said, intrigued. Blaze was a man of few words and didn't strike me as one who liked talking on the phone.

"Yeah. I was having my time with the Lord this morning, and He gave me a word for you. I don't know what it's about, or if it's even for right now, but I need to tell you today."

Standing, I paced my room, nerves cramping in my stomach as they always did when someone told me they had a word from the Lord. "Go on."

Blaze let out a loud exhale. "There isn't always going to be a perfect time for everything. If you wait until you think you're ready, the time will have passed you by, because how we measure our readiness is not how God measures it. You can't always think to yourself that there's a better time, because maybe the moment you're in is the best it will get for whatever it is that needs to happen.

"In our minds, we're ready when we think we can handle everything on our own, and that's far removed from what God wants. We're supposed to be completely dependent on Him, and sometimes that means stepping forward when we feel unprepared and underqualified."

Clearing his throat, Blaze paused, then added, "This making sense?"

Letting out a shaky exhale, I placed a hand on my stomach, the satiny material of my blouse cool against my warm hand. "Actually, Blaze, it does. And it's exactly what I needed to hear."

"Good," he replied. "Now go have a good day. Happy Thanksgiving!"

"You too," I told him, then hung up.

Crossing to the window, I gazed out over the front yard, watching the chickens meander around the front yard.

"All right, God," I sighed. "That's the third time someone's talked to me about the right timing. I get the point."

Sliding my feet into my slippers, I paused in front of the full body mirror propped against the wall in the corner of the room. Hair up in a messy bun with tendrils teasing my face, I'd opted for a makeup-free day, and the jade undertones of my blouse complimented my pale eyes.

Hearing Stetson call my name, a sudden flutter of nerves in my stomach had me turning away and heading for the door. I started down the stairs where he waited at the bottom, looking cheerful and relaxed at the same time. The red plaid shirt and dark jeans he wore looked good on him, but it was the gentle smile on his lips that captured my attention, and the sound of Frank singing along to Christmas music in the kitchen faded away for a moment as he held out his hand.

Reaching the last step, I took it, his calloused palm warm against my cold fingers.

"Misty," Stetson said, his voice low. "You look beautiful. I'm glad you're here."

Standing so close I could feel his body heat, I looked up into his familiar eyes, remembering the dance we'd shared so long ago. "Me too. Not exactly how I'd planned for it to go, but I wouldn't have it any other way."

Free hand dropping to my waist, Stetson pulled me even closer, eyes narrowing, dark hair falling over his tanned forehead. Clearing his throat, once, twice, he tightened his grip on my hand. "This isn't exactly how I imagined this moment but—"

A loud thump in the kitchen cut him off, and looking past him as he turned, I saw Frank sprawled out on the floor, spatula in one hand, mixing bowl rocking back and forth on the counter.

"Dad!" Stetson let me go, running to Frank and dropping down next to him. I wasn't far behind.

Kneeling on his other side, I pressed my fingers against his neck, feeling for a pulse as Stetson gently slapped his dad's cheeks.

"Frank?" I called, his pulse fluttering weakly. "Frank, can you hear me?"

Eyes slowly opening, Frank struggled to speak and Stetson reached for his phone that was clipped to his belt.

"I'm calling Jeff," he said, but Frank flapped his hand in the air.

"No need," he finally got out after his fourth try. "I'm fine. Blood sugar must have just gotten a little low, that's all."

"Dad, are you sure?" Stetson paused in dialing Jeff's number, worry twisting his lips, eyes wide. "You never mentioned having low blood sugar. Has this happened before?"

Frank tried to sit up, and I helped him. Stetson turned him so that he leaned against a cabinet by the sink.

"Once or twice," Frank admitted, a bit shamefaced. "Just means I'm going too fast."

"And yet you can run circles around me any day of the week and twice on a Sunday," Stetson gently mocked him, a muscle jumping in his jaw. "Dad, are you sure there isn't something you're not telling me?"

"Stetson, I'm fine. Just need to eat something, that's all," Frank assured him, legs stretched out in front of him, face a sickly gray color.

Watching him, I noted the sweat that beaded on his temple. The way his pulse pounded in his temple, the shakiness in his hands, the tremble in his voice—I knew he was holding something back.

Standing, I went to the fridge and pulled out some apples

from the fruit drawer, then grabbed some peanut butter from the cupboard.

"Stetson, help him to the couch, and I'll bring him some food and iced tea to get his sugar back up," I ordered the deputy. Turning a stern look on Frank I said, "We'll finish up dinner. You just take it easy on the couch and watch the game or something."

When he failed to protest, I shared a concerned look with Stetson before quickly slicing the apples as he helped his dad into the living room. Coming back into the kitchen, Stetson poured the tea, his usually steady hands shaking. Placing a hand on his forearm, I said a quick prayer.

Stetson looked down at me and gave me a weak grin. "I sure hope you know how to cook, because I have no clue about any of the stuff he's got going."

I shrugged, spooning peanut butter onto the saucer I'd filled with apple slices. "It can't be that hard, right?" Hearing a sizzle from the oven where the turkey was cooking, I let out a nervous laugh. "I can always call Aubrey."

"Guys, I'm just not feeling well—I'm not dead," Frank called from the living room. "I can tell you everything you need to know. Also, since you're already making me a plate, I could really go for that last slice of persimmon pie."

Chuckling, Stetson headed toward his dad, and just as he promised, Frank told us everything we needed to know about finishing up dinner. As we set the table, using the cranberry napkins and pretending not to hear Frank demanding we use the brown ones, Stetson and I joked around. The atmosphere was light except for when I accidentally bumped into Stetson when stepping back to admire our handiwork. Two candles he'd scrounged up added a cheerful glow to the room.

Hands on my shoulders, Stetson slowly turned me to face him, Frank's snores from the couch making us both smile.

Looking into Stetson's eyes, my heart thudded loudly in my chest as I memorized the way the hazel around his pupils was streaked with green. His left iris sported a freckle.

Face softening, Stetson slid his hands down my arms until he reached my hands. Holding them tightly, his brow wrinkled the tiniest bit, he took a deep breath.

"Moments like these are ones I've prayed for my whole life," he told me. Violin music filled the air from the radio in the kitchen as warm scents of nutmeg and cinnamon surrounded us. He wet his lips, still looking into my eyes.

"Never thought I'd get to this point. I've had my heart broken so many times—by girls, life, by my own doing—that I never believed this moment would happen."

"But God," I whispered, eyes filling with tears.

"Yeah," Stetson sighed. His words were halted by a loud snort as Frank woke up and turned on the TV, and the unexpected sound of football startled us both.

The moment broken, Stetson let out sigh. "Maybe we can revisit this?"

Giggling, I pulled away from him to go check the turkey and start mashing the potatoes. "We can sure try."

"Now THAT's what I call a Thanksgiving dinner." Frank leaned back in his chair, letting out a contented sigh.

I groaned, stomach tight against my waistband. "You just had to make three pies, didn't you?" I accused him. "It's like you knew I wouldn't be able to have just one slice."

"You had four, didn't you?" Stetson teased. "Two of the pecan?"

"Please," I scoffed. "You ate half the turkey."

Frank chuckled at our banter. "Keep it up, and you two will

have the dishes done in no time." Letting out a sudden cough, he took a swig of tea, hands trembling so much he spilt some on the tablecloth.

Forearms on the table, Stetson pinned Frank with hard stare. "Dad, I've been backing off every time you say you're fine, but I think it's time you tell me what's going on."

Setting his glass down, Frank leveled his son with an even harder look. "Oh, I'm sorry, I didn't realize that I report to you."

"Dad," Stetson said patiently, "I care about you. I have the right to know."

Frank let out a heavy sigh before looking away. "I don't think a holiday is the time to have this talk."

"I think whatever it is you need to tell me is going to be just as hard any other day," Stetson told him, and I went to stand, wanting to give them privacy, but Frank waved me back down.

"No, Misty, you need to stay. You're part of the family as far as I'm concerned." He waited until I was reseated before going on. "You're right, Stetson. I'm not doing so well. Been feeling under the weather the last few months, so I went to the doctor about three weeks ago." Looking down at the table, he picked up his fork and pushed pie crust crumbs around his saucer, the flickering of the candles on the table between us ebbing and weaving side to side as he blew out a breath.

Looking back up he finally said, "Son, I don't know how to say this, but it wasn't good news."

"What is it?" Stetson said, leaning forward, his voice quiet with restraint.

"I have cancer, and the doctor said—"

"Cancer?" Stetson fell back in his chair, face going pale. "Dad, are you sure?"

Frank nodded. "They did all the tests. Doctor said ... doctor said I might see Valentine's Day, but I might not." Voice pained, he looked at us, clearing his throat. "See why I didn't want to tell you today? I don't want this to be your last Thanksgiving memory with me."

"You can't have cancer." Stetson's voice trembled. Glancing at me, his eyes were wet. Looking back at his dad he went on, "Dad, I can't lose you too."

"Stetson," Frank began, but Stetson shook his head, shoving his chair back so hard it scraped the floor.

"No," he said vehemently. "No. I—I can't." Turning, he left the room, the sounds of the front door opening, then slamming shut reaching our ears a moment later.

Biting my lip, I stared at Frank. "May I ask what kind?"

"My lungs," Frank replied tiredly, scrubbing a hand down his face. Chest heaving, he began to pray, reaching across the table toward me. After a moment, I took his hand and joined him.

It's hard knowing what to pray in moments like those, and I fell back on scripture, repeating the praises that David penned in the darkest times of his life. It was only when Frank squeezed my hand that I stopped.

"You're such a beautiful woman of faith," he whispered. "And you're here for such a time as this." He squeezed my hand again. "Now go out there and see to my son. I've some highlights to catch up on for the game."

"But," I protested.

Frank gave me a stern look. "Nope. I'm fine. Made my peace with this already. So go talk to Stetson." Winking at me, he broke the solemn moment. "And remember what I said about timing."

Standing, I took a deep breath before going to the foyer and slipping on my sneakers and one of Stetson's hoodies that hung on the coat rack. The temperature had dropped when the sun set. Muttering a prayer for courage under my breath, I opened the door and crossed the dark yard to the barn, where I wrestled the heavy side door open.

STEPPING INSIDE, I paused for moment to let my eyes adjust to the light, the smell of hay, horse, and feed a shock to my nostrils after spending my day smelling food.

Stetson sat on a bale of hay under the loft, head in his hands. The faint nickering of the horses in their stalls almost drowned out his quiet prayer.

"God, why?" he whispered, and a tear slipped down my cheek at the pain in his voice. "God, why would You allow this? He's such a good man. Why would You take him this early? I don't understand. And I don't think I can do this. Not my dad ... not my dad."

Looking up at the rafters for a second, I bit the inside of my cheek, then walked over to Stetson, feet shuffling through loose bits of hay. Sitting down next to him, I wrapped my arm around his shoulders. My free hand rested on his knee.

Turning, he pressed his face into my shoulder, his tears hot against my skin as he wept, railing against God but also trying to praise Him. Tears slipped down my cheeks as I held him as tight as I could, wishing I could ease his pain. No words came to mind, so I kept silent, knowing that sometimes, just being there for someone is more important than any number of platitudes.

We stayed like that for a long time, and running my fingers through Stetson's thick hair, a song rose to my lips and I hummed it. Immediately, the presence of the Comforter filled the barn, and I opened my mouth and softly sang, asking God to let the rain of heaven fall, to open the floodgates and have His way.

Sniffling, Stetson pulled away from me and joined in, his voice raspy with pain. Our voices blended together, rising and falling as God moved, His peace and mercy descending on us. Stetson raised his hands, standing, and I followed suit, tears coursing down my cheeks and dampening the neck of my hoodie.

"Your will, Your way, Lord," Stetson whispered. Voice breaking, he paused for a moment before going on, "I trust You, God. I hate the road You're leading me down, but I trust You. Though this hurts more than anything I've ever been through, I know that You are good and perfect in all Your ways."

I took up his prayer as he began to weep again. "Oh Lord, You are good." Pausing, I wiped my damp eyes. "Great is Your faithfulness to us, and Your foundation is firm. God, we praise You, and we trust You. Let Your presence fill this barn, let it fill Stetson's home. Have Your way in our lives and let this situation bring glory to Your name."

We continued to pray and worship a while longer, and after we'd been silent for moment, I turned to Stetson. "Whatever you need, I'm here."

Meeting my gaze, his eyes bloodshot, Stetson nodded. "I know," he whispered, wiping his face with his shirt sleeve. "This is hard, but I know now, no matter what happens, everything is gonna be okay, even if it's not my version of okay."

"God's plan is perfect," I reminded him. "Even if it doesn't seem like it."

"Speaking of perfect," Stetson said, voice hoarse, "I'm starting to wonder if it'll ever be the perfect time for us."

Stepping closer to him, I raised an eyebrow after letting out a sniffle. "Funny thing about that. There isn't."

Stetson gave me a puzzled look, his nose slightly red. "There isn't what?"

"A right time," I told him. "As people have been telling me

repeatedly, there isn't going to be a perfect, or right time. We're never going to be ready, so we just have to go for it." Taking another step forward until I was right in front of him, I placed my hands on his chest, feeling his heart beat steadily under my palms, I looked up at Stetson.

"I love you," I whispered. "And I want the moments we just shared to be the blueprint for our future."

Stetson drew in a sharp breath, hands going to my waist as his eyes darkened, and I went on. "Is now the right time for this to happen? Maybe not, but I don't think there is a perfect time for something like this. I don't want to keep waiting and then one day turn around and realize I've lost twenty years because the timing was never on point. I don't want to miss this—you, us, a future together."

Stetson pressed his hands against my back, pulled me against him, and looked down at me. "Misty, I've always known you were the one for me. And I want what just happened to be our future too. I love you, and I'm sick of waiting for life to be good to have you in it."

Standing on tiptoe, I kissed him, the salt of our drying tears mixing as our lips moved. Smiling against my kiss, Stetson slid one hand up, twisting his fingers into my hair, and I pressed a hand against his cheek, tracing my thumb over his jaw, his stubble rough under my touch. Warmth flooded me as the feeling of finally being as close to home as I could be while still on earth filled my heart.

With Royce and his cohorts in police custody Stetson and I finally admitting our feelings for one another, I could only breathe a prayer of thanks. While we still had the battle of Frank's cancer before us, I knew that with God by our side, there was nothing we couldn't handle.

The slight twisting in my stomach that warned me not all was at it seemed was quickly soothed when Stetson looped his arm around my waist as we headed back to the house. Giving myself a quick shake, I forced away anxious memories of when we thought Aubrey was safe when the killer was actually among us.

But no matter how hard I tried to believe the FBI had captured everyone involved in Ryan's murder and my own attack, I couldn't shake the feeling that someone was about to announce checkmate, and it wouldn't be us.

12

"A spring wedding sounds beautiful." Aubrey's voice was dreamy as she swirled a bite of buttermilk pancakes through maple syrup before putting it in her mouth.

"Perhaps a double wedding?" Lacey teased, flipping through a salon supply catalog. Next to her, Jenni deftly twisted earring wire with pliers, small containers of tiny beads in front of her.

"Now that would be something," Brey sighed, resting her forearms on the table. "Two best friends marrying their Prince Charmings. Y'all have such different styles, but they would mesh so well."

"Now wait a minute," Terri protested from across the kitchen as she poured herself a cup of coffee. "Aren't we getting ahead of ourselves?"

Weak sunlight filtered through the windows of the kitchen in Aubrey's bakery, which was closed for the day. My growing group of friends decided to meet for an impromptu supper and had spent the last two hours devouring Aubrey's hashbrown bowls and pancakes while catching up on everything that happened over the holiday.

"Just a bit," Aubrey agreed. "I'm not engaged."

Sipping my lemon tea, I gave her a look, and said in a pragmatic tone, "Yet."

"True, but we aren't talking about marriage as seriously as you and Stetson. Sounds like all you've left to do is go buy a dress and secure a date with Pastor Brent."

Blushing, I set my mug down. "We figure since we've known each so long, why wait? I know he's the one I want to spend my life with, and he feels the same about me."

"Have you discussed rings?" Jenni fixed her gentle gaze on me and set her earring set down to accept the cookie Brey offered.

"No," I answered. "Ladies, it's only been a week since he proposed, and we've both been a bit busy."

"Blaze said the paperwork from the case has become overwhelming," Aubrey said, smoothing the front of her green hoodie. The faint scent of her strawberry perfume tickled my nose, and I took a deep breath of the familiar smell.

"What about Ryan's girlfriend?" Brey asked. "Seems like she showed up for breakfast that one morning and then just disappeared. Poor thing needs some counseling and rehab."

"She needs more than that," Terri mused. "A good dose of God, I'd say. But don't worry, she's still here. Holed up in her hotel room. Cade said two of his agents interviewed her three times, but there's no evidence she had anything to do with Ryan's death, or even Misty's attack." Shifting in her chair, Terri bit the bottom of her lip. "She might be trying to dry out."

"No better place than here." I leaned back in my chair. "I just think that so much of what happened could have been avoided if Ryan had simply gone to Blaze as soon as things went south instead of doing the whole code thing in the books and putting so many people in danger."

"Seems easy to say he was scared senseless. But I think he was covering up for someone, and I don't think it was Royce." Lacey's voice was quiet as she stared at me, almost as if she'd been feeling the same unease that had settled into the back of my mind for the last week.

"We'll probably never know," Terri answered. "The FBI closed the case, and I think we shouldn't worry about it."

"Respectfully, I disagree," Lacey said.

Brey and Jenni fell silent, having been looking at pictures on Brey's Instagram. Terri set her coffee cup on the table, and Aubrey mirrored her actions.

"Why is that, Lacey?" she asked. "What do you know that we don't?"

Lacey sighed, gray eyes meeting mine for a moment before returning to Terri's. "The night I had Royce over so that Misty could brea—I mean, look around Ryan's apartment, I kept sensing that while he was up to no good, he was also not in charge. Almost like he was on puppet strings, if that makes sense."

"So you think the mastermind is still on the loose," Aubrey said.

Lacey nodded. "Exactly."

Terri swirled the coffee around in her cup. "I'll pass this on to Blaze, but I think we're all just a little nervous because of everything that happened with Mabel."

Face darkening momentarily, Aubrey pushed her plate away. "All right ladies, enough talk like this." Leaning forward, she placed her forearms on the table. "What I want to know about is all the gaps Terri has in her story about Frank. Seems to me like she's the one hiding something."

Brey clapped her hands together. "Ooh," she squealed. "Maybe a triple wedding?"

Jenni stared at her, picking her pliers back up. "Girl, you've got weddings on the brain."

Brey shrugged. "Better than murder."

"Well, if we're gonna talk about me and Frank, then we need to talk about Lacey and Cody," Terri defended herself.

"Why drag me into this?" Lacey protested, bracelets clinking together as she pressed a hand to her chest. "I've nothing to hide."

Pinning her with a steady look, I quirked an eyebrow. "Sure about that?"

Blushing, Lacey lowered her hand. "You saw that whole thing with Cody behind the salon, didn't you?"

"I'm confused," Jamie announced, selecting a few beads from the dish in front of her.

"Yes," I admitted. "Stetson and I both did. It was when he was helping me pack to leave for his ranch."

"I thought I heard someone laugh during the middle of it all," Lacey mumbled, picking up her coffee cup and staring into it.

"Ladies," Jamie interrupted, perplexed, "do you care to let the rest of us in on what you're talking about?"

"That would be nice," Brey agreed while Terri chuckled.

"Well, obviously, Terri already knows," Lacey grumbled, sending me a glare.

Raising my hands in surrender, I could only grin. "You know I tell her everything."

"Fine," Lacey huffed, setting her cup down. "If y'all must know, Cody asked me to take him back two days before Thanksgiving."

"I do hope you told him no," Aubrey interjected, biting into a muffin. "That boy is nothing but trouble, Lacey, and he'll only break your heart again."

"I sent him on his way," Lacey assured her, giving me a warning kick under the table when I opened my mouth to add in that she'd slapped him.

"But you still have feelings," Jamie stated.

With a sigh, Lacey nodded. "Yeah, unfortunately."

"The best thing to do is keep you two in prayer." Terri's eyes were kind as she studied the blond salon owner. "Matters of the heart are always difficult, no matter your age. The two of you would make a beautiful couple if Cody would grow up a little, if you don't mind my saying."

"It's not that he needs to grow up," Lacey answered, wrapping her fingers around her coffee cup while Brey shifted in her seat. "It's that he needs to confront his demons."

"Let's say he does." Jamie frowned at the earring in front of her. "Would you take him back?"

"Within in a heartbeat," Lacey told her. "But he's pretended to change before. and I've fallen for it."

"We can pray about that too," Aubrey told her. "God delights in moving in our most painful situations and bringing light to the darkness."

"Amen to that," Terri sighed.

Looking at her, Lacey raised a perfectly shaped eyebrow. "Now that you're done deflecting, why don't we talk about you and Frank?" she asked sweetly.

Laughter filled the room when the dispatcher turned pink.

"So, maybe it will be a triple wedding," she said.

"This has been going on for a while, hasn't it?" Jamie guessed, and Terri nodded.

"A few years, yes."

"If he's anything like his son, you couldn't be making a better choice," I told her, my tone slightly dreamy.

The sigh Terri and I shared sent our friends into giggles, and the tension that crept up on us quickly dissipated. The rest of the evening was spent discussing engagement rings, the importance of a good cologne, and Aubrey's new waffle recipe.

"Release into child's pose and take a moment to reflect as you give your back a break." Voice low and soothing, I walked between the students of my 10 a.m. class. "Trust in the Lord with all your heart. All of it. Not some of it, but all of it. Even the broken parts."

Stopping next to Abigail, who had signed up for the class the day before, I bent, pressing my hand onto her lower back. "No arching here, Abigail," I reminded her. Noticing the space between her bottom and her heels, I made a mental note to send her home with a stretch guide packet. Streaks of paint stained her forearms, and there was a bit matted into her messy ponytail. Obviously sore from renovating her store, she gave a short nod at my words, letting a sharp exhale as she attempted to deepen her stretch.

Straightening, I continued pacing between the twenty-three women, stopping here and there to adjust forms, offer encouragement, and even pray when I felt the Spirit's nudging. Once class was over and I'd seen my students off, I locked the front door to my studio and made my way into the kitchen.

In the five days since Thanksgiving, Stetson and I had spent every spare second cleaning and repairing the damage left by the men who assaulted me. The countertops I'd ordered to replace the ones they destroyed would be here any day, and except for the deep cuts in the current ones and the smell of fresh paint lingering in the air, it was hard to believe my kitchen had been a crime scene not even two weeks ago.

The criminals had broken almost all my dishes, and my new ones were on backorder, so Aubrey loaned me some from her diner. I carefully placed a bowl on the island before filling it with homemade yogurt. Going to the fridge, I grabbed the container of fresh strawberries Jesse sent over the day I'd returned from Stetson's ranch.

Just as I placed the strawberries in a strainer to be rinsed in the sink a knock sounded on the front door. Padding back across the kitchen and through the studio, I stopped when I saw Cynthia, Ryan's girlfriend, standing outside. Thin shoulders drooping, she stared at her sandaled feet, frizzy hair pushed behind her ears.

The hesitancy that filled me upon first seeing her eased as the Spirit nudged me forward, and sending up a quick prayer for discernment, I unlocked the door and pushed it open.

"Cynthia." I studied the woman in front of me for a moment before stepping back to allow her to enter.

Locking the door behind her, I turned to face her, surprised to find her green eyes filled with tears that quickly overflowed and slid down her sore covered cheeks.

"I need help." The words were quiet but the anguish was clear, and lifting her hand, the young zookeeper showed me the Bible she was holding that I hadn't yet noticed. Mouth opening, she went to say more but I cut her off and turned toward the kitchen.

"Come with me," I told her. "Let's have a snack and a talk."

Falling in step behind me, loud sniffles filled the room as I led the way. Once we entered the kitchen, I sat Cynthia down at the island and filled another bowl with yogurt and topped it with the strawberries I quickly rinsed.

Sitting next to her on a stool with the cushions slashed open, I placed one hand on the Bible she'd set on the counter and the other on her shoulder.

"Now, what do you need help with? Since you've brought a Bible, I'm assuming it's of a spiritual nature."

Spooning yogurt into her mouth like she hadn't eaten in weeks, Cynthia nodded even as a tear plopped onto the countertop. Her pert nose, lightly dotted with freckles, was red, and her lips were chapped and smeared with drying blood. Scratch marks traced up and down her bare arms, and the loose jeans and faded grocery store blouse she wore reeked of cigarettes, air freshener, and something I couldn't quite place.

"They told me over at the hotel that you're a counselor, and I think you're the only one who can help me." Finally meeting my eyes, Cynthia clasped her hands in her lap. "Misty, I've down something really bad, and I don't know what to do. I was reading this Bible that was in my hotel room, and I didn't know where to start. The beginning seemed kinda boring so I just flipped to a random page, and this is the first thing I read."

Lips trembling, Cynthia opened the Bible to where she'd stuck her hotel key and pointed to a well-known verse. "I kept rereading it, and no matter how hard I tried to move onto the next piece, it's like it kept calling me back." Voice breaking, she began to sob. "And I kept hearing this really quiet voice say 'No more condemnation, Cynthia. No more shame. I'm here to give you freedom.'"

"And you don't know who it was or what it meant," I finished for her, smiling even as my eyes stung with tears.

"Well, yeah."

Wrapping my arm around her trembling frame, I pulled her closer.

"That is the voice of the holy God calling your name." Tightening my embrace as shivers went through the young woman's body, I softened my voice. "I've seen a lot in my years as a counselor, and I think you've a bit of a substance problem."

"You could call it that," Cynthia whispered.

"Do you want to be free from it?"

"Yes." The words were quiet, the body that uttered them shaking almost uncontrollably, but the will was firm.

Turning to completely face the young woman, I clasped her hands in mine and waited for her to meet my eyes again. "May I pray for you?"

"So, you spent your day teaching yoga, praying with Cynthia and getting to see God move in her life? Shucks, all I did was fill out some end of year paperwork and figure out what to get Terri for Christmas."

Voice nonchalant, Stetson's body language was anything but, and his hazel eyes were narrowed.

"Well, yeah." Hands clasped together in my lap, I stared at the man I was going to marry as we sat on the small couch in my living room. "She wouldn't say why she thinks that or who it might be, but she was very clear that I should be careful."

Stetson sighed. "And did you tell her that if someone's watching you, they saw her come to you?"

Nodding, I let out my own sigh. "But no matter how much I urged her to tell me, or come to you for safety, she insisted she's safer going back to Houston and going to rehab to restart her life. And maybe she's right."

"And maybe not," Stetson replied, one hand resting on my knee, the other running through his hair. "But I can't force someone to tell me anything or accept my help." Picking his phone up from where it sat on the coffee table, he tapped the screen before holding it up to his ear.

"Cade? Yeah, it's Stetson. Listen, I just got a tip that there might be one or two more guys out there." Pausing for a moment, a frown creased his forehead as he reached for his coffee cup, removing his hand from my knee. "No, I don't know who it might be. Cynthia, Ryan's girlfriend, is the one who gave the tip, but she's declined to elaborate." Taking a sip of his drink, he nodded. "Right. Great. Thanks. Yeah, you too."

Hanging up, he looked over at me. "Cade's on it. Said he'll try to track Cynthia down and have a talk with her, see if he can get her to tell him who she thinks is still out there."

"And here I'd been thinking we'd made it through everything and can sit back and enjoy the holidays after getting your dad settled in." Tone dry, I picked up my cup of lavender tea, thinking of all I had to get done in the next few weeks to prepare for Christmas, my wedding, and, most importantly, helping Stetson move Frank into his guest bedroom as his dad started cancer treatment at a nearby cancer center.

Stetson's gaze softened and he placed his hand back on my leg. "Have I told you how much I love you?"

Nodding, my cheeks flushed as I put my hand on top of his. "Only a thousand or so times." Twisting to face him after setting my tea down, I smiled. "And it's something I'll never tire of hearing, just so we're clear."

"Good. Because I intend to tell you that every day for the rest of my life," Stetson replied, leaning back, crossing one leg over the other. The warm light of the living room lamps threw his face into shadows for a moment as he shifted and my heart skipped a beat as I studied him. So much had changed in the last few weeks, and it was still hard to believe how many dreams God was making come true.

"Speaking of life," Stetson finally went on after a long pause, "have we decided on a ring? Or at least a day to go look at them?"

The rest of the evening was spent looking at different styles of engagement rings on various websites and discussing wedding plans, Frank's cancer treatment, and, of course, how long we thought it was going to take Blaze to propose to Aubrey.

Despite Stetson insisting I spend the night with Aubrey since there was a slight chance of danger, I decided to stay home and bid him goodnight after we prayed together.

I was still smiling from his parting kiss as I readied for bed and brushed my teeth. It wasn't until the lights were out and the covers were pulled up to my chin in my newly redone bedroom that my pulse finally returned to a normal rhythm.

No matter what happened, I knew that with God in control, everything would work out for my good. Focusing on that thought, I slipped into a peaceful sleep that comes only from trusting in the One who does all things well.

"DON'T you think you're moving a bit fast there, kid?" Seth's eyes squinted as he stared at me while Jesse scanned the groceries he placed on the counter.

"Not at all," I replied, giving him a grin. "Stetson and I are both adults who know what we want, so why wait? Why have a long engagement if we're sure of each other?"

Seth glanced at Jesse. "What do you think about it, Jesse?" he asked the grocery mart owner. "You've been married. Don't you think this is kind of sudden?"

"Not really my place to say," Jesse replied nonchalantly, quickly typing in the code for the bag of lemons Seth handed him. "Especially since I'm divorced, but," he paused, counting the lemons, "if they think they're ready, might as well go ahead."

"Well," Seth sighed, pulling out his wallet, the whir of the coolers behind us loud, "seems like I'm outvoted. Guess I just don't want to see you hurt, Misty."

"And for that, I'm thankful, Seth," I told the older man. "Kinda makes me feel special to know you're looking out for me."

"Someone's got to," came the muttered reply as Seth input his pin number. "Kids these days."

Jesse and I shared a look as Seth grabbed his bags and left the store without another word. It wasn't hard to see the toll Ryan's death and Royce's arrest had taken on him. His usually straight back slouched, his steps were slower than they had been two weeks ago, and the dark circles under his eyes hadn't escaped me.

"Well," Jesse broke the silence, "despite what Seth thinks, I'm happy for you, Misty. You deserve a happily ever after."

Placing my items on the counter, I studied my friend. "Do you ever wish for someone, Jesse? Someone to spend the rest of your life with? Or are you content with your store?"

"Now don't start analyzing me," Jesse laughed as he grabbed my bag of pasta. "I'm completely satisfied with my life, thank you very much."

"You still miss her, don't you?" Tone gentle, I reached across the counter and rested my hand on Jesse's. While Vicki's death was a blow to us all, it'd been exceptionally hard on the shopkeeper, who had once carried a flame for the bakery owner.

Jesse stilled, looking down. "If you weren't my friend, I'd toss you out," he said. "But, yeah, I still miss her. Always will, I suppose." Scanning the pasta, he placed it in a bag before grabbing the carrots I offered him. "But what's done is done. She's gone, and it's time to move on."

"It's all in God's time." Making a mental note to spend

some extra time in prayer for my friend, I squeezed his hand. "Trust Him, even when things don't work out how we want them to."

"Any maybe that's for the best," Jesse whispered.

Ten minutes later, I made my way home, struggling to carry the many bags Jesse packed my groceries in and regretting not taking him up on his offer to help me.

I reached my studio and fished my keys out of my pocket. Locking the door behind myself, I quickly put everything away before loading the dishwasher and hitting the start button. The sound of someone knocking on my back door reached my ears, and I put my cup down.

Crossing the kitchen, I opened the door, surprised to see Seth. Standing back, I ushered him in.

"Seth! Is everything okay?" Closing the door behind him, I followed him back into the kitchen where he sat down on one of the stools.

"I need to talk to you, Misty." Voice low, eyes wet, Seth stared at me, and I wondered if today would be a repeat of yesterday with Cynthia.

"Okay." Drawing the word out, I leaned against the counter by the fridge and stared at him. "What's on your mind?"

"This will stay between us?" Seth shifted on the stool, jean clad legs rubbing against each other as he hooked the heels of his boots on the rungs.

"Of course," I replied, puzzled. "Nothing leaves this room, provided you haven't murdered someone or have thoughts of self-harm."

Letting a deep breath, Seth ran a hand through his white hair. "God forgives people, right? When they do things that they shouldn't, even if the thing was terrible?"

"Not gonna lie right now, you're kinda scaring me, but yes,

God forgives people if they repent and turn from their sin." Crossing my arms over my chest, I stared at the old man. "Seth, have you done something?"

"And if I did murder someone?" he blurted out, cutting me off. A chill went down my spine, quickly followed by beads of sweat pooling at my lower back.

Pushing away from the counter, I went and stood in front of Seth, studying him. A slight shimmer on the floor caught my eye and looking down, I saw something glint up at me as it caught the kitchen light. Bending, I picked it up. No bigger than the back to an earring, it was a shard of blue porcelain.

Jaw tight, I straightened, looking back at Seth as memories of the night I was attacked flooded my mind, quickly replaced by the moment Jeff extracted pieces of blue glass from the wound on my back. Glass that was the exact match for the shard I now held and was much like the pieces that had dotted Ryan's shop floor after I'd knocked over a blue flamingo.

"Oh, Seth," I whispered. "God forgives us, He truly does. But if we have the opportunity to right the wrong, we should."

"But what if that would mean losing everything?" Tears dripped down Seth's weathered cheeks as he spoke and my breath caught.

"To follow after Christ means to deny ourselves. It means to leave everything behind, to lose it all, so to speak, pick up our cross, and follow after Him."

"Some would say that's too high a price after what they've done." Seth looked down.

"To live is Christ, to die is gain," I said softly, touching the piece of glass in my palm with my finger even as my hands shook. "Truly the greatest thing we could ever experience."

Seth looked back up at me, as if sensing my racing heart. Noticing my eyes darting to my phone where it sat on the counter by the sink, he slid off the stool while reaching behind him.

"I'm too far gone for that," he said, and bringing his arm back around, he pointed a gun at me that he must have had concealed in his waistband.

"I'm so sorry, Misty."

A calmness came over me, a gentle whisper in my ear reminding me that I wasn't alone, and my shaking subsided. Looking straight into Seth's tired eyes, I swallowed hard, stepping away from my phone.

"You don't have to do this." Pausing, I licked my lips before going on, acutely aware of the loudness of the dishwasher as it entered its heavy cycle. The scent of lavender essential oil wafting from my diffuser suddenly stung my nose.

"At this point if you plead guilty, you'd have a chance at a light sentence, and you know it. But if you through with what you're planning right now, there's no going back. Ever." Voice quiet, my breath caught on the last word.

Seth shook his head, brows coming together as his lips thinned. "Twenty years behind bars at my age isn't gonna happen, Misty. They'll give me life, and I'll die in there." Blinking hard, he reached out to steady himself against the counter with his free hand. "No. I'd rather have the guilt of your death on my hands and be free in another country than go to prison."

"And what of Cynthia?" I countered. "Will you hunt her down? Somehow go after all the men you'd hired to take care of her and me? And what of Stetson? He'll figure it out eventually, and you know Texas has the right to extradite from Mexico."

"There'll be no need," Seth answered me, the gun wavering a bit as his hand shook. "From Mexico I'll catch a flight to Venezuela, a country that rarely extradites, and will soon just be another face in the crowd."

Waving the gun at me, he motioned to the stool I stood closest to. "Have a seat. It'll be easier to make sure you're dead that way."

Slowly, I made my way to the stool and sat, the torn leather cushion cold against the backs of my legs. I clasped my hands in my lap. Looking up at Seth, I relaxed my shoulders. This wasn't the way I had planned on dying. Rather, I'd hoped for a life spent with Stetson while we pursued God together while building my business and helping Stetson build his. I had no intention of not seeing the next sunrise, the next Sunday, or even the next thousand.

"Two things before you go through with it," I said softly. "That's the least you can do."

Seth lowered the gun but continued to stand. "Let me guess," he said with a sigh, boots scraping the floor as he shifted his weight, "Why?"

"That's the first thing," I replied. "I'll tell you the second after that."

"If you haven't noticed, Misty, times are hard. And when times are hard, people do what they have to do. For me, that meant going back to a trade I once excelled at as a younger man."

"Drug running," I inserted.

Seth clenched his jaw, looking away for a moment. "Yes. Not something I'm proud of, but I grew up in the slums of Houston watching my mother prostitute herself out just to provide food for her family while my father rotted in prison for being on the wrong side of a gang shootout. I started out young, only seven or so, when my mother began to use me as a mule. By the time I was sixteen, I was head of my own circle."

"But you left." Rubbing my hands down my yoga pants, I shifted on the stool as sweat dripped down my back.

"My mother died when I was twenty-four, and shortly after that, the police really came down hard on the drug cartel. It was too dangerous to continue my lifestyle. At that time, I had no interest in taking my business to Mexico. So I left. There was more than enough in savings to live pleasantly for several years, and I even invested some of it. Realty, bonds, you name it, I tried it. And it worked. Until it didn't."

"What happened?" Question genuine, I could only pray that someone would sense I needed help before it was too late.

"The crash of 2008. I lost everything, and I do mean all of it. Suddenly, my investments were gone, the housing market went down, and I found myself with more debt than I could ever hope to pay off, even with a fulltime job, so I turned to the only thing I knew would never fail me, no matter the state of the world. Drugs. Regardless of how poor an economy may be, there will always be a market for illegal substances. Always. People will be starving but will find money for a fix."

"The recession was difficult for everyone," I said. "For some, it was harder than it was for you, yet they didn't turn to selling drugs, getting people addicted to them, or possibly being responsible for the resulting deaths."

"Are you calling me weak for going back to what I know?" The gun came back up.

I lifted my chin, looking Seth straight in the eye. "Yes, I am. And if you thought I wouldn't, you clearly never knew me as well as I'd believed."

The gun lowered, Seth seemingly surprised at the sudden heat that filled my tone, and he gave me a slight smile. "Fair enough. Judge me all you want, but I did what I had to."

"How did Ryan and Royce get involved?" I asked, heart still slamming against my chest from the sight of the gun moving. "Especially Ryan."

"Ahh, my boys," Seth sighed, looking over my shoulder into the distance for a moment as he reminisced. "I've known those two since they were in diapers when they moved next door with their parents. They were adorable as toddlers and menaces as teenagers, but it was obvious from the moment I first met them as they moved in that they were extraordinarily smart children.

"It was an honor to be a part of their lives as they grew, and my wife and I often watched them when their parents worked. They became like grandchildren to us and were even pallbearers at my wife's funeral." Seth paused, blinking as tears filled his eyes at the mention of his late wife. "We never lost touch, even after they'd moved out and gone their ways. Both went to college, Royce for sales, and Ryan for engineering. And they excelled, but they always came home when they could."

A tremor went through the older man, and he sat down hard on the stool behind him, the breath leaving his lungs in a whoosh. It was in me to question if he was unwell but considering he was pointing a gun at me, it was obvious he was ill in more than one way, so I remained silent.

"It was never my intention to involve them, but I needed help about five years ago, and the jobs I gave them weren't without perks. Ryan needed money to finance his research and continue his studies, and Royce was in severe debt from a messy divorce that cost him everything except for the clothes on his back and the car he was sleeping in."

Tone dry, I interrupted him. "So you decided exposing them to drugs and all that the illegal substance world entails would help them."

Seth laughed, the sound harsh and grating, pale eyes holding a bit of a twinkle. "Always the smart mouth," he said. "But, yes. Neither were interested in the drugs, and it was actually Ryan who suggested we switch to running cocaine and meth. That was part of the reason why he opened his shop in the first place."

I held up a hand, palm out so that Seth didn't think I was trying something funny. "And Royce provided the containers, which you disguised as souvenir flamingos." Pausing, I remembered Stetson telling me about the K-9 finding traces of cocaine on the floor of Ryan's store. "Blue flamingos, specifically, that Royce would paint himself. You would deliver them, full of drugs, to Ryan's store, where customers would stop in and buy them."

"Exactly," Seth said, tilting his head, crossing one leg over the other as if we were having a normal conversation and he wasn't about to kill me. "He made the flamingos himself, casting the porcelain around the baggies, effectively creating an airtight seal that even the best of K-9s can't smell through. All the time he spent in college paid off, because he created different streams of revenue should the IRS or FBI ever look our way, explaining away our income."

Seth's chested heaved with a heavy sigh. "Unfortunately, Ryan started to make a name for himself in the physics world and wanted out. And in this business, there can't be any loose threads."

"And my attack?" Voice low, my anger was evident. "The blue glass Jeff pulled out of my back? Was I just another 'loose thread' that needed to be snipped?"

"It was done on my orders, but no, I wasn't physically part of it." Seth looked down. "I know you won't believe me, but that's the thing I regret the most. Hurting you never should have happened, and for that, I am sorry."

Biting my lip, I clenched my hands together, the tattoo on the underside of my wrist catching my eye, and I stared at it.

"I trusted you, Seth." The sudden onslaught of tears in my eyes caught me off guard and they dripped down my cheeks and landed on my bare arms, causing goosebumps to rise. "We all did, and we loved you."

"Some people are born to be trusted, others are born to disappoint," Seth said quietly. "It's my destiny."

Shifting, he coughed. "Look, it's been nice finally being able to explain everything to someone, but—"

Head jerking up so fast a tear flew off my nose, I glared at him. "No! You promised me two things. You've only fulfilled one."

Making a disgruntled noise in the back of his throat, Seth rolled his eyes. "You can only prolong the inevitable for so long, Misty." He relaxed. "But go on."

"Thank you," I said, a bit of bite coming into my tone as I entered a more familiar territory. Meeting his gaze, my own was unwavering as my jaw tightened, a strength that wasn't mine filling me. "My second request is that you let me pray for you."

Jaw dropping, Seth stared at me, clearly taken aback. "Not sure if this is a delay tactic," he said slowly, "since you know Stetson is out at Jamie's, or if you're that much of a Jesus freak."

Smiling, I lifted my chin even more. "It's the latter if you must know."

Shaking his head in disbelief, Seth made a wide gesture with his free hand. "Then by all means, pray away. God's not going to save you."

"We'll leave that up to Him," I replied calmly. "And I said I want to pray for you, not for myself. I'm secure in where I'm going. You're not, and I want to change that."

Slouching, Seth waved his hand again as he looked around the room. "Please just get it over with, I still have to kill you and make my flight."

Sudden fear filled me at his words but a warm touch to my shoulder, though no one stood behind me, immediately calmed me, and opening my dry mouth, I did the only thing one can do in such a situation. Pray.

"God." My voice was strong and I lifted my chin. "God, thank You for this very moment, for this even now time with Seth."

At the mention of his name, Seth's head whipped around and he stared at me, chest rising and falling rapidly, grip tightening on the gun.

"I ask not that You save me, but that You save Seth. Save him from himself, from everything he's struggling with. Even if it's not right now, Lord, save him."

"Stop," Seth cried, his finger stretching toward the trigger of the pistol. "Misty, shut up!"

Voice filled with fear, he turned the gun on himself, pressing the end of the barrel against the underside of his jaw.

"I'll kill myself if you don't stop! I swear, Misty, I'll do it." Sweat poured down his face, a vein bulging out from his forehead, but even as his words were threatening, his tone was pleading, begging for help.

Ignoring him, I got to my feet and stood in front of him, and though my voice faltered, I continued to pray. Seth stared up at me as if I'd lost my mind, and maybe I had. But when tears began to fall down his cheeks, running down the gun and dripping to the floor, I knew I couldn't stop.

Reaching, I placed a hand on his shoulder, the gun lowering until it rested in his lap. Only inches from my hip, all it would take was a quick tightening of Seth's finger to kill me.

"Misty," Seth whispered, and meeting his reddened eyes, I paused. "Misty, help me."

"Don't ask me." I squeezed his shoulder. "Ask God."

"Jesus." Seth stopped, stammering a bit. "Please help me."

Shoulders shaking as he sobbed, Seth covered his eyes with

his hand, and after a moment, I slowly reached out and took the gun from him, placing it on the island.

Breakthrough in the spiritual sense is both a beautiful and messy experience, and the more trauma, the bigger the mess. Seth had experienced much pain in his life and the prayers that left his lips broke my heart.

We stayed like that for a long time, the dishwasher finishing its cycle, and it wasn't until the front of Seth's shirt was damp with tears that he finally quieted. Bloodshot eyes looked up at me, holding a glimmer of peace, and reaching up, he cupped my shoulder with a trembling hand.

"What now?" he asked.

"That's up to you," I replied. "But I'd suggest doing the right thing."

"Like turning myself in?" Twisting, Seth picked up the discarded gun, and my breath caught for a moment before he stood, holding it at his side.

"Yeah, something like that."

Seth held the gun up, and we stared at it, then at each other, both realizing the gravity of what just happened. Neither of us heard the door behind me open.

"Drop your weapon, Seth!" Stetson's voice filled the room as he stepped in and saw Seth holding a gun, and whirling, I saw him stop in the doorway, pointing his pistol at Seth.

"Stetson, no!" I tried to step in front of him at the same moment Seth startled, dropping his gun.

The shot was loud in my small kitchen, and the sudden flash of heat by my foot had me jumping back even as Stetson tried to step to the side. The bullet caught him just above the hip, sending him back into the wall as he let out a surprised grunt.

"Shots fired! Shots fired!" he yelled, a red stain blooming across his shirt. "I need backup!"

"Stetson, wait," I cried, throwing myself in front of Seth as the older man crumpled.

"You told me to drop it, so I did," Seth's voice was panicked even as he landed on the floor while Stetson slid down my freshly painted wall that now sported a bullet hole and streaks of dark red blood.

Running to Stetson, I fell to my knees next to him. Gun still pointed at Seth, he pressed his free hand against his wound, his face steadily losing color. Placing my hands on his arm, I pushed down as hard as I could, but despite the fact he was bleeding everywhere, he refused to lower his gun.

"Stetson, he dropped it. It was an accident." I pushed harder, and after a moment, sweat trickling down his forehead, Stetson lowered his arm.

Blaze rushed in. Seeing Seth passed out, head half under one the stools, he turned his attention to Stetson, holstering his gun. Quickly pushing me to the side, he knelt by his deputy, one hand pressing a button on his cell phone while the other went to Stetson's collar.

"I've got a gunshot victim," he said, setting the phone on the floor.

"Be there in two minutes." Jeff's calm voice filled the room.

"Copy that," Blaze replied. Placing both hands by Stetson's neck, he ripped the wounded officer's shirt open, buttons skittering across the floor, some landing in the pool of blood by my hand.

"Don't strain yourself," Stetson croaked out, trying to make a joke, but his weak smile quickly turned into a grimace when Blaze pressed down on his wound. Gaze flickering to me, he reached out with a bloody hand and cupped my cheek, eyes only slits as he groaned in pain.

"You know I love you," he said, and I nodded, reaching up to cover his cold hand with mine.

"And I love you," I whispered, tears falling from my eyes and trickling down our hands. "More than life itself."

"Besides God, you're everything to me, Misty." Stetson stopped, drawing in a harsh breath, eyes squeezing shut. Hand falling away from my cheek, his head lolled to the side, and a cry escaped my lips.

"He only passed out," Blaze said, still tending to Stetson's wound. "He's not dead, nor is he dying, despite the way you two were carrying on."

"I'm starting to think your bedside manner is always going to be lacking." Jeff's deep voice cut Blaze off as the young doctor entered the room, black bag in hand. Motioning for Blaze and me to move, he knelt next to Stetson, snapping on a pair of gloves. Looking over at Seth who had passed out, he quirked an eyebrow.

"One of you mind checking on him? Might be a heart attack."

Blaze crawled over to Seth and felt the elderly man's pulse before checking his pupils. Seth groaned, one leg drawing up as he did so and Blaze looked over at me.

"Nope. He's fine."

"Fine as one can be in his situation, anyway," I muttered, turning my attention back to Jeff as he hovered over Stetson.

"Never who we think it'll be, is it?" he said, brows drawn together, hands slick with blood as he focused on the deputy.

I sighed. "Unfortunately."

The sound of tires crunching on the gravel behind my building reached our ears and looking past the open door, I watched an ambulance from the county over pull up. Suddenly dizzy, I put my head between my drawn-up knees, the blood speckled on them a flashback to not so long ago when Ryan was hit just outside my door.

Two paramedics entered my kitchen, looking a bit

surprised at the sight of not one, or even two people on the floor, but three.

Jeff gave them a shrug. "He's our gunshot victim," he said, motioning to Stetson with his chin, hands still pressed to Stetson's side. "The elderly gentleman passed out. He may have an underlying concern and will need to be restrained pending an investigation."

"What about her?" the younger looking paramedic said, gesturing to me, dark brows raised.

Jeff shook his head. "Just an upset stomach."

The smile I sent the paramedic from my place by the island counter was weak, and Blaze patted my knee as he moved to sit next to me.

"Aubrey's going to drive you to the hospital," he said softly, watching the medics work on his friend. "Cade will meet you there and get a statement when you're ready."

Leaning my head on his strong shoulder, I started to cry in earnest. "I'm afraid, Blaze."

Turning, the once ill-liked sheriff pulled me into his arms, pressing my head against his chest, stopping me from watching the medics place Stetson on a stretcher after stabilizing him, an IV line now running from his arm.

"I know," he said softly. "But Stetson is one strong guy, and though it looks bad, he'll be okay."

Arms tightening around me, he rubbed my back as I sobbed. Stetson's blood on my cheek stained his tan shirt.

"I can't do this anymore, Blaze. I can't."

"You never had to." Resting his chin on my shoulder, Blaze sighed, voice rumbling in his chest as he spoke. "God is with us, Misty. Always has been, always will be, and even though we can't feel His presence, trust me, He's here right now."

A cool hand pressed to my back, the scent of brown sugar,

bacon, and maple syrup suddenly surrounded me, and turning, I flung myself into Aubrey's flour dusted arms.

Shuddering, I clung to my friend as she and Blaze exchanged a few words before he left, following the medics as they carried Seth out, boot heels loud on my wooden floors.

Aubrey pushed me away from herself. Her blue eyes met mine. "Do you want to change before we leave? It'll be a bit before they'll let you in to see Stetson, and you know they keep the waiting rooms cold."

Throat too tight to speak, I gave her a weak nod, and helping me to my feet, she led to my bedroom where she dug through my closet. Handing me jeans and a hoodie, she let me change before taking me into the bathroom and washing the blood off my face.

"It's gonna be okay, Misty," she said, hands gentle as she scrubbed at a stubborn spot on my cheek. "You're in shock right now, but it's gonna be all right." Hugging me, she left the room, giving me a moment to collect myself before joining her outside where we crossed the street to her bakery and climbed into her Jeep.

The ambulance had already left. Blaze stayed behind in my kitchen to secure the crime scene, and a crowd gathered outside the front of my studio. Lacey and Jamie were among the concerned bystanders. They both waved at me, and the smallest of smiles touched my lips as Aubrey backed the jeep out of its spot and aimed for the highway.

"Not to pry, but if you need to talk, please do. If not, I understand," she said, setting the cruise control before reaching out to fiddle with the heat dials.

"Maybe in a minute," I said, staring out my window at the plains that were passing by in a blur.

"It's over, Misty. You made it."

Though Aubrey spoke the truth, it did little to assure me,

because no matter how hard I focused on the passing scenery, all I could see was Stetson sliding down the wall, blood dripping on the floor. The memory of his dark eyes fluttering shut replayed in my mind, and a sharp coldness filled me.

Despite everything that happened in the last few weeks, and even in the last year with Mabel murdering Vicki and attempting to kill Aubrey, and then the attack in my kitchen, I'd never been more afraid than I was right now.

13

"I can't say for sure, as I'm not a judge, but since Seth took advantage of a young adult he'd known since they were a child, who had been in dire financial straits, Royce's sentence shouldn't be too bad. Most likely ten years." Cade's voice was warm and reassuring as he sat next to me in the private waiting room the hospital let us use.

Looking into the FBI agent's green eyes, I tried to give him a smile. "On one hand, I'm glad to hear that, because everyone deserves a second chance, but on the other hand, I wish Royce would go away forever. The amount of people he hurt due to running drugs is innumerable."

Cade nodded. "I know. And I understand a lot better than you think." Reaching out, he rested a hand on my arm.

Aubrey filled a paper cup with water from a fountain that grumbled when she pressed the button on it.

"Thank you for giving me your statement right away. It's tough, but it really helps me get the ball rolling for everyone else."

"And what will happen to Seth? Once he's medically cleared?" Aubrey sat down in the chair next to me and pressed the flimsy cup into my shaking hand.

Cade looked down at the tablet balanced on his slacks-clad knee. "Well, with all the info Misty gave me, and the fact Seth has denied to wait for a lawyer and has been telling anyone who will listen all his crimes, he'll be placed in jail with no bond. A case this big usually goes to trial fairly quick, and with the crimes he's connected to, definitely life without parole."

Taking a sip of the chlorinated water, I wrinkled my nose. "Were you ever able to locate Cynthia?"

"Not yet." Cade tapped a button on the tablet, closing the window he'd been using. "But we will. From everything we've been able to find, she's an innocent girl who got hooked on a drug her boyfriend was selling."

"Did you find out who was behind the hit and run?" Aubrey asked. Seeing me shudder at the mention of it, she wrapped an arm around my shoulder, crossing one leg over the other.

"Seth ordered it, according to Royce," Cade replied. The dim light from the lamps in the room highlighted the shadows under his eyes. "And Royce carried it out."

"Killed his own brother because of drugs," Aubrey murmured. "My word, this world has fallen."

"Money, not drugs," he corrected her. "Money is always at the root. But you're right. That's a pretty dark thing to do."

A gentle knock on the door interrupted him. Opening, it revealed a petite nurse wearing scrubs covered in cartoon characters. "Misty?" she said, and when I stood, she smiled at me. "Stetson is awake. Would you like to see him?"

"Oh, yes, please!" Scurrying toward her, water sloshed out of the cup I still clutched.

Letting a chuckle, she took it from me. "Right this way,

then," she said, and led me down a series of hallways until we came to a small room. Opening the door, she ushered me in, shutting it behind me.

I paused for a moment and stared at Stetson where he lay in the hospital bed that was slightly inclined. His six-foot-plus frame seemed small, the faded hospital gown he wore and the rough looking blanket covering his legs almost swallowing him. Mouth drawn in at the corners, his face was pale, and the wave he sent me, one finger connected to a pulse reader, was weak.

Shaking myself, I cautiously made my way to his side, careful not to touch any of the machines that surrounded his bed. The soft beeps they made sent a shiver down my spine.

"Hey." Looking up at me, his eyes squinted at the corners. He tried to smile.

"Hey." Voice a hoarse whisper, I held back tears as I reached out and touched his cheek before smoothing his hair away from his forehead.

"Are you in pain?" I asked, noting the dullness in his eyes and the IV drip next to the bed.

"Nah," he replied, words slow. "Can't feel a thing. Kinda want a burger, though."

"Probably not gonna happen for a while," I told him, smiling at his attempt at humor. "But I promise I'll get you one as soon as they say I can."

"I love you," Stetson said, reaching out with his free hand.

I sank to sit on the edge of the bed and took his hand in mine. His callouses were rough against my skin, and I tightened my fingers over his when he flexed them.

Opening my mouth to repeat what Cade told me, I was cut off by a knock on the door. A doctor, who looked to be in his mid-fifties, entered the room. He quietly closed the door behind him, holding a clipboard against his chest.

"Ahh," he said, meeting my gaze. "You must be the fiancée." Crossing the room, he stopped at the foot of Stetson's bed.

"I'm Dr. Walsh. I operated on you, young man." The look he gave Stetson was stern. "You should be more careful, son."

Stetson gave him a weak thumbs up. "Thanks," he whispered. "I'll try."

Dr. Walsh looked down at his clipboard, tapping a sneakered foot on the floor. His dark blue scrubs made a rustling noise.

"You lost a lot of blood. The bullet went clean through, thankfully, so I didn't have to rummage around for it. Sometimes with abdominal gunshots, the bullet can get lodged by the spine and cause a whole lotta problems, so I was glad it went out your back."

"When will I get outta here?" Stetson shifted a bit, grimacing. "Got a wedding to plan and horses to train."

Dr. Walsh glared at him. "It'll be a while before you're discharged, and a lot longer after that before you're cleared to ride a horse." He paused. "If you ever can, that is."

"And what does that mean?" Despite my efforts, the tremble in my voice was obvious.

Dr. Walsh looked at me over the top of his rimless glasses for a long moment before answering. "Too soon to be completely sure, but ..."

Looking back down at the clipboard, he flipped through the pages it held before looking back up, and Stetson gripped my hand so tightly it hurt. "But what?" he asked. "But what, Doctor?"

Dr. Walsh finally looked back up, sighing. "It looks like you've got some partial paralysis, Stetson."

Stetson's sudden intake of breath was loud. and he looked down. Tears came to his eyes, slipping down his cheeks.

Glancing back at the doctor, I asked the question Stetson couldn't. "How bad? Or is it too soon?"

"Left side, from the waist down. It's too early to tell if it's temporary or permanent. He wouldn't have noticed yet because the effects of anesthesia are still wearing off."

"All because of a freak accident." Stetson's voice was slightly bitter as he shook his head.

Holding the clipboard down by his side, the doctor gave us a sympathetic smile. "Not what you wanted to hear, I know, but you *are* alive, Stetson. Don't take that for granted." Dr. Walsh looked at me. "And your fiancée happens to be a yoga instructor. That will most certainly come in hand with your therapy."

Tapping the edge of the clipboard against the railing at the foot of Stetson's bed, he cleared his throat. "Things are never as bad they seem. I've had patients come in and it was total paralysis, but one, two years later, they've regained full mobility. Like I said, this is all preliminary."

"Thank you," I told him, stroking the back of Stetson's tense hand. "It's just a lot to take in."

"Of course," came the kind reply. "If you have any questions, feel free to ask Meg, your nurse, or ask for me. Once Stetson's healing is underway, we'll get him set up for therapy." He left the room, and suddenly it was quiet, save for the quiet hums and beeps of the machines around us.

Stetson stared at our clasped hands for a long time before speaking, and I ran my fingers through his soft hair while I waited, tracing his jaw before letting my hand drop.

"Remember that night in the barn?" Tone soft, he looked up, brown eyes dark and slightly bloodshot. "How we prayed about my dad's cancer, and God just ..." Trailing off, he covered our hands with his other one as his voice broke. "God just filled the atmosphere with His presence. And even though we had no idea what the future held, and we still don't, there was peace?"

Sniffling, I swallowed hard, my throat suddenly dry. "I remember."

Stetson let out a shaky breath, more tears sliding down his tan cheeks. "Let's do it again, Misty. Let's get to that place again."

So we did, and suddenly, I knew that everything was going to be more than okay. It was going to be amazing. As long as I let God be in control, no matter what was going on, no matter how I felt, the outcome would be more fulfilling and beautiful than I could ever hope or imagine.

Three Weeks Later

"Misty! Can I get a comment on the outcome of today in the courtroom?"

"Misty, is there anything you'd like to say to the press about the proceedings?"

"How do you feel about how the case is being handled so far?"

Head down, I pushed through the crowd, Stetson next to me in his wheelchair. Blaze held onto the handles tightly as he maneuvered through the crowd of reporters gathered outside the courthouse in Houston.

"No comment," he bit out repeatedly, running over the foot of one reporter who got a little too close with a microphone.

To my left, Cade repeated his words as he urged me forward, one hand on my back as he pushed people away.

"Make some room, people," he said, flashing his FBI badge.

Some of the press fell back, but just as quickly, others took their place.

Moving his hand to my arm, Cade gripped my elbow, steadying me when I stumbled, the heel of my black pumps catching on uneven concrete. The light rain that fell from a dull gray sky was cold on my neck, and I was thankful Aubrey insisted I wear her black trench coat. Its thick material protected me from the biting wind that suddenly came up, wafting the heavy scents of perfume, cigarette smoke, and city filth into my face.

The story of a seventy-something year old drug runner with a very colorful past, attempted murders, and Stetson's injury, had overtaken the news for the last several weeks, and Flamingo Springs was overrun with press and onlookers alike.

Thanks to Seth willingly sharing everything he could remember as well as Royce confessing to his part in the drug running, the case was progressing quickly, and today was the first of many days in court. It was expected to drag out for at least a month, and I could only pray it wrapped up sooner than that, as today alone left me exhausted.

Cade opened the door to the SUV that had chauffeured us from our hotel to the courthouse. I bit back a yawn. Life had been a hectic blur since Seth's arrest. Between taking Frank to his cancer treatments, a task that Terri helped me with when she could, and spending as much time with Stetson as possible, I barely had time to study the books his physical therapist gave me, as well as continue to run my business and YouTube channel.

Leaning my head back against the seat, I looked to the side and smiled at Stetson as he buckled himself in. Cade placed his wheelchair in the trunk, and Blaze climbed into the passenger seat.

Feeling my gaze on him, Stetson looked up and grinned.

"Not what we'd had in mind for December, is it?" he drawled, chuckling when I blushed and slapped his arm.

Twisting in his seat, Blaze looked at us, raindrops rolling down the sleeves of his jacket as a steady drizzle pattered on the windshield. "And what does that mean?"

Stetson grinned, smoothing the tendrils of hair that escaped my chignon behind my ear as I looked everywhere but at Blaze.

"Oh," he said, "nothing much. Just that me and Misty kinda planned on getting married this month before everything happened."

"Huh." Obviously surprised, Blaze stared at us. "Is that so?"

"Is what so?" Cade asked, sliding behind the wheel and cranking the engine.

Blaze jerked his thumb toward Stetson and me as he faced forward again. "These two kids were planning on elopin'."

Cade laughed, meeting my gaze in the rearview mirror, green eyes squinting as he spoke. "Kids these days."

"Not were—*are*," Stetson murmured for my ears only, and dropping his fingers from my cheek, he grabbed my hand.

Sliding across the seat, I snuggled into his side while Cade drove us home. My head resting against Stetson's shoulder, and he wrapped his arm around me, holding me tight. While there'd been no change in his paralysis, Stetson's wound healed quickly, and he usually used a crutch instead of a wheelchair now.

Sighing, I closed my eyes. The sound of his heart beating under my ear while his breath stirred my hair lulled me into a doze.

Although the future from our human perspective seemed uncertain and at times overwhelming, we'd decided to trust in a God who was certain in all His ways, and both of us were excited for whatever came next.

Our happily ever after wasn't turning out how I'd thought,

or even hoped it would. In many ways, it was almost a letdown, but the bonds Stetson and I were forming as we faced trials together were more important than a perfect engagement or wedding, and I wouldn't change a thing about how everything was turning out.

As sleep claimed me and the sounds of the SUV's engine faded away, I smiled, knowing I was right where God wanted me. And there was no place I'd rather be.

ACKNOWLEDGMENTS

Thank you to Diane Burns for letting me bounce idea after idea off you and send you snippets of scenes at 2 a.m. to critique. Your encouragement, support, and care packages made this book possible. I wouldn't be where I am without you, as a writer or a person.

ABOUT THE AUTHOR

Keri Lynn discovered her love for writing before she even entered first grade, and that passion has only grown over the years. She has had several poems published as well as a fantasy novel and plans to continue expanding her genres. When the Wisconsin born writer isn't busy creating new worlds, she can be found experimenting in the kitchen, writing music, and exploring waterfalls. She resides in Nashville, Tenn.

PANCAKES, BACON
& A SIDE OF
MURDER
KERI LYNN

time is running out and she must discover who is behind the attacks before she joins her dead competition.

MORE MYSTERIES FROM SCRIVENINGS PRESS

The Plot Thickens

by Susan Page Davis

Skirmish Cove Mysteries - Book Two

Jillian only wants to redecorate one room at the Novel Inn—

but first she has to deal with murder.

Murder strikes Skirmish Cove during the coastal town's winter carnival. Jillian Tunney, part owner of the nearby Novel Inn, discovers the body of a clerk at her favorite bookstore. With her sister Kate and brother, Officer Rick Gage, she tries to find out who killed him.

Meanwhile, Jillian is immersed in redecorating one of the themed rooms, but Kate is annoyed when a mysterious guest at the inn doesn't want to leave his room. The innkeepers find they have way too many secrets to solve.

The Case of the Innocent Husband

by Deborah Sprinkle

A Mac & Sam Mystery - Book One

Private Investigator Mackenzie Love needs to do one thing. Find out who shot Eleanor Davis. Or else.

When Eleanor Davis is found shot in her garage, the only suspect, her estranged husband, is found not guilty in a court of law. However, most of the good citizens of Washington, Missouri, remain unconvinced. It doesn't matter that twelve men and women of the jury found him not guilty. What do they know?

And since Private Investigator Mackenzie Love accepted the job for the defense and helped acquit Connor Davis, her friends and neighbors have placed her squarely in the enemy camp. Therefore, her overwhelming goal becomes to find out who killed Eleanor Davis.

Or leave the town she grew up in.

As the investigation progresses, the threats escalate. Someone wants to stop Mackenzie and her partner, Samantha Majors, and is willing to do whatever it takes—including murder.

Can Mac and Sam find the killer before they each end up on the wrong side of a bullet?